For Kim,

Determined to Obey

CJ Roberts

Copyright © 2014 Neurotica Books LLC., CJ Roberts

All rights reserved.

ISBN-10: 1502885417

ISBN-13: 978-1502885418

License Notes

This book is a work of fiction. Names, characters, places and incidents are products of the author's imagination or are used fictitiously and are not to be construed as real. Any resemblance to actual events, locales, organizations, or persons living or dead, is entirely coincidental.

Copyright © 2014 Neurotica Books LLC., CJ Roberts
www.aboutcjroberts.com

All rights reserved. No part of this book may be used or reproduced in any manner, including translation, whatsoever without written permission, except in the case of brief quotations embodied in critical articles and reviews.

Edited by: Kayla Robichaux
(kaylathebibliophile.blogspot.com)

Cover design: Amanda Simpson, Pixel Mischief Design
(amanda@pixelmischiefdesign.com)

DEDICATION

For every person in my life who makes my days worth living.
Should you all leave me one day, I hope I'm not far behind.

Preface
PLEASE READ
A note from the Author

This story was originally written for inclusion in the anthology *Pink Shades of Words*. All of the proceeds went to breast cancer research. My gratitude goes out to all of you who purchased a copy and contributed to this wonderful cause.

This story has been edited to allow for prior knowledge of the *Dark Duet* plot and all of its characters; I had to avoid spoilers in the anthology as much as possible. Whether you're reading this story for the first time or not, I hope you'll enjoy what I've done with it.

I love all of my characters, but some of them really speak to me, and I've always had a little bit of a soft spot for "Kid", the nineteen-year-old biker with a tender heart. In fact, I had originally written a small love triangle involving Kid, Livvie, and Caleb. Kid was meant to be a character Livvie could relate to, someone her age who'd lost someone he loved and had been taken captive. It sure as hell didn't hurt that he and Caleb share so many physical attributes. However, in the end, I just couldn't justify another hundred pages to an already enormous second volume.

That said, having a beautiful boy held captive in a house with a hedonist couple like Felipe and Celia was simply too much temptation to resist. **FAIR WARNING – ALL SEXUAL PAIRINGS APPEAR IN THE TEXT.**

***

The character "Kid" appears in both *Captive in the Dark* and *Seduced in the Dark*.

This novella takes place in Mexico and follows Kid after he and his girlfriend, Nancy, are taken hostage by a group of men led by Caleb. Unbeknownst to Kid or Nancy, they are taken to the mansion of Felipe Villanueva, an eccentric crime boss with a taste for the taboo.

Wrongfully accused by Nancy of the attempted rape and subsequent assault of Caleb's escaped captive, "Kitten", Kid is tortured by his captors.

We join Kid in the dungeon, where he is about to meet Felipe and his companion Celia for the first time…

1. Kid

He's alone, absolutely alone...lost! He's never been lost. He's never wondered if he'll ever see his family again. Kid is eight years old; he's terrified for the first time in his life. His eyes look everywhere at once, but he can't see her. She should be there—on the bench—waiting. He wasn't gone very long, he thinks, but can't be sure. How big is the park? Where is she? Where is his mama? His tongue darts out across his upper lip: Salt. Dust. Desperation. He cries out, sudden and fierce, "Mama!"

No answer.

An old man turns to look at him, and every warning he's ever been given about strangers—strange men especially—sings through his blood. Kid has been told how beautiful he is, warned he's a temptation, and been given the talk about people who like to touch underwear parts. So when the old man takes a step toward him, Kid runs.

He runs, but has no idea where he wants to go. He just has to keep moving, searching, calling out—whatever it takes to find her. If he stops moving, he'll fall down and start crying. His dad says there's never been a problem solved by crying.

He thinks about going back to the skate ramp to see if the boys he met left, but he knows they did. He only came back because they were leaving. He can't remember where his mom parked the car. What if it's gone? He brushes the thought away—his mother would never leave him.

"Kid!" his mother yells. He knows it's her without having to lay eyes on her. Relief slams into him so fast he isn't ready. His knees buckle and land on the soft grass at the same time his butt

hits his ankles, and he cries. He cries loud and hard until his throat burns and his stomach cramps.

His mother lands on her knees in front of him. He screams as his narrow arms are crushed within his mother's grip—she's never hurt him before. She gasps apologetically and rubs his arms. Her hands inspect him, checking and rechecking imagined wounds. She's out of breath—she's crying too.

"Oh, Kid...oh, God, thank God! I thought I'd lost you," she says between sobs and messy kisses. Satisfied he isn't hurt, she runs her fingers through his sweaty, blond hair, and then presses her nose to his scalp and inhales. She wipes tears from his crystal blue eyes and stares into them in the way only a mother can—like he's the only thing that has ever mattered—like she'd die for him—like she'd kill.

Kid soaks in his mother's love like a flower absorbs light, by turning toward it. He allows himself to cry within the cocoon of her embrace, because there are indeed some problems that can be solved by crying. He knows there will be consequences for running off, and yet it seems unimportant. His mother loves him, keeps him safe, and that's all that matters.

"Don't cry, baby," she sings into his ear and rocks him.
..."Don't cry."

2. Celia

The boy won't cease whimpering. It breaks her heart a little. She drags her fingers gently through his hair and holds him. "Don't cry," she whispers in his ear. Her English isn't very good, but she knows enough to get by. She'll have to become fluent if she plans on keeping her new pet.

"I'm sorry," the boy replies, and leans into her touch. He's delirious with thirst and quaking with fear. "I was all alone." He licks a dry path across his upper lip. His nose wrinkles in distaste—presumably at the flavor of his own dry blood. "I love you, Mama."

Celia's chest pangs. There have been many nights she has longed to be called Mother, but it is something she will never be. It's a pity this boy can never go home again. He must love his mother very much; it's a sentiment she only vaguely empathizes with, never having known her own mother. "Shhh, *pobresito.*"

3. Kid

Kid knows that word. It means 'poor baby' or something like that. He frowns; his mama doesn't speak Spanish. A prickle of awareness penetrates the thick soup of his consciousness—he's dreaming. It's very important he not wake. He burrows deeper into the eleven-year-old memory of his mother's arms, of the last time he was lost and then found. She's found him again. She'll take him home. *Home is the road. No...that's not right. Home is...*

His home is gone.

"Don't leave me," Kid whispers. His chest hurts. Vaguely, he comprehends there's more hurt yet to be catalogued, knows he's been hurting for a while. He shakes his head; a whine escapes him. *Don't open your eyes.*

A man speaks. Kid begins shivering, because only bad things happen when he hears male voices. Realization creeps over him like quicksand sucking him down into his body and into the present.

He is no longer eight years old.

His parents are long dead.

The last of his family was murdered in front of him.

He and Nancy have been taken as hostages.

They were beaten.
Nancy betrayed him.

4. Felipe

At first, Felipe wanted nothing to do with Rafiq's mess. He's never met Rafiq's apprentice Caleb, and has not once felt inclined. But things change. Powerful men get older and rest on their laurels. Felipe has always been patient in waiting for these moments. Moments like this one.

He can use this young man to get information on Caleb. There's plenty Felipe already knows, but one can never know too much about their allies or enemies—especially as one can often become the other, the enemy of my enemy and all that.

So when Rafiq asked—quite imposingly—if Caleb could make use of Felipe's plantation, he acquiesced. Had he known Caleb was going to allow his kidnapped slave to escape and cause her captor to slaughter three men, start a fire, take two hostages, and bring them to Felipe's house in Tuxtepec—his *home*—he may have been less gracious. It's been two days and Caleb has yet to arrive with *Kitten*. The men Caleb sent ahead of himself have been occupying themselves with the hostages. It will be their undoing.

It was assumed the boy and his companion were part of the plot to hold Caleb's slave for ransom and attempted rape, but they have since learned the boy is apparently innocent—of the rape, at least. It's fortuitous for the young man. His female companion, on the other hand…she isn't faring so well. Celia abhors rapists with a fervent passion, and she has no sympathy for women who turn a blind eye to the cruel lusts of men. And yet...she wants to subjugate this boy. Celia is a complex woman. Regardless, he won't deny the young man is... alluring. "Do you know why you're here?"

5. Kid

Kid can't suppress his dry sobs. "I don't know anything!" he yells. The words are barely audible. He's screamed himself hoarse over the last however many...hours? Days? He thinks he's been here at least a day or two. Time gets away from him between beatings.

They're going to kill him soon. He really doesn't know anything. He's less than useless—a burden. His kidnappers won't let him live, not after they've already killed so many others. *Abe. Joker.* His mind shies away from the last name, but his heart throbs with loss anyway. *Uncle Tiny.*

The man in the room is still speaking, but Kid is too lost in the maze of his frantic thoughts to behave with any bravery. He offers whimpers in place of words. *Please don't let me die like that.* At first he'd thought Caleb's absence a good thing, but Kid quickly learned the men they'd been left with were just as vile. Despite his fear, he attempts to open his eyes only to discover he can't.

He knows he's dead already. Isn't a man allowed to beg for mercy in his final moments? After all, there's no one left to be ashamed of him.

***

"Jair. Knife."

DETERMINED TO OBEY

Kid can't even scream. He's trying. Every sound he attempts is trapped inside him. There's a gun in his back and a fist in his hair holding him on his knees. His uncle Tiny is only two or three steps away, sprawled face-down on the shitty carpet, blood dripping from his broken nose.

The words register the moment Caleb straddles Tiny's back and yanks his head back to expose his tense neck. "Jair. Knife."

Uncle Tiny struggles. It's over before Kid can scream.

"I warned you, you motherfucker!" Caleb sneers. He's full of rage and he proves it.

Blood sprays across Caleb's chest, neck, and face, but the psychopath has enough sense to close his mouth and turn away—but only for the first arch. As he turns back and keeps stabbing, ripping, and separating head from shoulders, Caleb's eyes never leave their mark—as though he knows the blood will only continue to slow.

Kid still can't scream. Warmth runs down his left thigh as he watches his uncle's blood spread out across the floor like living black ooze. You pissed yourself, *his mind supplies. He's surprisingly calm about the whole thing. He's staring at his uncle's head and it's not on his shoulders.* That's so weird. *He has a thought about horror movies.* All the severed heads he's seen are suddenly unrealistic. *Then he wonders what those thick white pieces holding part of his uncle's head on are called.* Sinew? Where've I heard that before? Health class? Is someone screaming? *It's them; it's all of them: Kid, Abe, Nancy, and even Joker, they're all screaming.*

Caleb smells like hot copper and raw meat. The tip of his knife is suddenly poised beneath Kid's chin. "Stop screaming or I'll cut your tongue out." *Kid sucks his lips into his mouth and bites down to muffle himself. He's dizzy with panic and lack of oxygen.* "Now," *Caleb smears Tiny's blood across Kid's cheek with the flat side of the blade,* "tell me again what happened."

Kid knows the moment he opens his mouth all he'll be able to do is scream. Distantly, he acknowledges the rest of his friends are attempting silence as well. The attention is on him alone. His bladder clenches, but he's already wearing his piss. He cries instead. His uncle is dead and he can't spare him a thought. He's too afraid of what comes next.

It isn't until Caleb takes hold of his hair and tilts his head that Kid's survival instincts finally kick in. "I helped her! P-p-p-please," he sputters. He pulls in gulps of air. It's not enough. His world is dark around the edges. "I swear. I—"

"—helped her. Right. You helped her after *your buddies raped her, after they beat her and broke her bones!" He presses the knife under Kid's chin hard enough to produce a trickle of hot blood.*

This is it, Kid thinks. He closes his eyes to wait for the pain. "I swear," he whispers. "No rape. I helped her." Abruptly, he's caressed from one corner of his eye to the other. The gentle touch is a shock; something sinister lies beneath. The caress is followed by another; he can taste his own tears and his uncle's blood across his bottom lip.

"You swear," Caleb says. He snorts derisively. "Kid, I'm going to take you and that little bitch over there with me, and when Kitten wakes up, she's going to tell me what happened. Understand?" The younger man opens his eyes just in time to see the back of Caleb's hand approaching. His cheek lands in a blood-soaked patch of carpet.

"Jair," Caleb's voice is cold, "take this little pussy and the girl alive. Kill the rest and burn the house down." Caleb drops the knife and doesn't look back as he makes his way toward the bathroom.

Kid is numb. His uncle is dead. Abe is bleeding out. Joker is going to burn. Kid doesn't want to think about his and Nancy's fate. As Caleb walks past with the girl cradled against his chest, Kid can see a familiar pain. They're both about to lose everything.

Caleb kisses her forehead softly, tenderly, as though he isn't the same man who just decapitated someone with a knife. "Don't worry, Kitten. I promise I'm going to make it better."

***

6. Celia

Despite her new pet's distress, he continues to shift closer to Celia. He's a needy little thing; though honestly, he's not little at all. He has to be over one and a half meters tall…taller than Felipe. The thought makes her smile inwardly.

The boy's body is wracked. He sobs incessantly and with good reason as his bruises will attest. Rafiq's men are complete brutes, but neither Celia nor Felipe had a way of knowing whether or not the young man was dangerous or a rapist until earlier that day, so they were not predisposed to offer aid. Poor boy, she thinks, so terrified. Celia feels a tiny bit guilty for the ember of arousal taking shape in her belly. She can't get enough of his naked vulnerability; Felipe would never be as open. She coos in the boy's ear, soothing him with softly spoken words and gentle touches.

"Felipe," she says in their native tongue and fixes her master and lover with an admonishing glare, *"you're scaring him."* What had he been doing with such vile people? His companion, the blond woman, is retched, and Celia took great satisfaction in hearing her scream. Imagine! A woman holding another woman down while others attempt to take her virginity—Celia is furious every time she thinks on it. Perhaps some time with men of similar predispositions will teach her a valuable lesson about loyalty. Not only did she deny her involvement, she

implicated the rest of the boy's motorcycle club, effectively marking them for death. Rafiq does not allow for loose ends.

Celia will not allow the young man in her arms to become another tied end, and neither will Felipe. The boy is valuable for more than one reason.

7. Felipe

Felipe smirks; Celia is smitten. "What is your name?" he asks the boy. He attempts to keep his tone free of judgment or disdain, not quite sure how he feels about Celia's fascination with the other man, whom, Felipe admits, is quite beautiful and suited to both their predilections. However, there is a fine line between pet and partner, and Felipe won't let anyone divide Celia's heart.

"Kid," the young man says, mostly mouthing the word. "Water? Please?"

"Did you rape the girl?"

"No." Kid clenches his jaw. Felipe knows he's been asked the question ad nauseum, and it amuses him that the younger man continues to deny the allegations despite everything. "No," Kid pleads. "I keep...I keep telling you. Please. Where am I?" He sobs, too dehydrated to produce tears.

"You're still in Mexico. I have many homes, but this is my favorite. I'm a little disappointed they brought you here, to be honest. Torture is often necessary, but I prefer not to sully my home. Are you certain you're not a rapist?" His words are spoken with all the gentleness of a hammer striking a nail.

"Felipe," Celia snaps, *"stop toying with him! You'll only make it more difficult."*

Felipe laughs. "My Celia has taken a liking to you, boy. What do you think of that?"

"Water," Kid barks and subsequently flinches. *"Mmmsorry,"* he slurs, *"thirsty. Needsomewater."* His tongue snakes out to lick his dry lips repeatedly until Felipe takes pity and goes to retrieve a bottle of water from the small Frigidaire he keeps nearby. The boy makes pleading noises at the sound of the cap being removed and groans lustily when Felipe holds the bottle to his lips. Felipe watches the long line of the younger man's throat as he swallows with renewed energy and clear desperation. "More! More please," he begs after the water is pulled away from his mouth.

"It will make you sick," says Felipe.

"I don't care," Kid gripes.

"I care." Felipe's tone has gone from amused to authoritative.

Kid shuts his mouth and nods. He lets his head fall against the wooden beam at his back in defeat. "I'm sorry. Thank you." He sounds better already.

"Kid," says Felipe, "what is it you want most?" He presses a finger to Kid's lips before he can speak. "Out of life, I mean."

8. Kid

Kid's adrenaline spikes. Whenever anyone speaks to him about living, it's a prelude to threatening to kill him. He's always loved the club's rides into Mexico. The food is incredible, the women eager, and bouncers never card him. Every month for the last two years, he and the rest of the Night Devils have come into Mexico to hang for a week, pick up their drugs, and head back across the border. Not this time. This time, Tiny fucked with the plan and it cost them everything.

"You gonna kill me now?" He tries to sound unafraid. Death has to be better than the torture, he tells himself. He fears the knife though, is *terrified* of the fucking knife, and he hopes they'll just shoot him in the head before he knows what's happening. Quick and painless—that's how he wants to die. Well, he wanted to die an old man on his bike, going ninety-miles-an-hour down a dark stretch of road, but a bullet will have to do. He tries to bury himself in the memory of his mother's embrace—*home*—he wants that to be the last thing he thinks about.

Abruptly, feminine lips press gently against Kid's own. He pulls away in shock. Felipe's laugh filters through his ears as an amused rumble. "I can kill you if you wish it. Though, I was going to suggest the opposite. Would you like to live instead? Would you like to get out of this room?"

Kid licks his dry lips. He's exhausted. He's hurting. And he has no reason to lie—especially when he has no cause to believe he'll be set free. "I want to go home."

9. Celia

Celia presses against Kid's side. "Where is home?" she says in English. Her voice seems to soothe Kid somewhat. She lifts the bottle of water to his parched lips, allowing him one large sip and nothing more.

"With my parents," Kid whines. He shifts in his bonds, craning his neck to tuck his head in Celia's neck. She can't resist nuzzling his sweat-damp hair with her cheek as she cords her fingers through his tangled hair. "They're dead," he whispers.

Celia whispers her condolences while continuing to stroke Kid's hair and quietly asks how they died. She never knew her mother and has always rejoiced in the death of her father, but she can still empathize with Kid's heartache insofar as she understands love itself.

"Car accident," he replies in monotone. "Five years ago." His lips brush Celia's neck as he speaks; it makes her shiver. "I should've gotten a clue when I had to use my key to get in the house. Mama was usually home. She used to make me a sandwich, ask about my day, shit like that." His stomach growls. "She wasn't there. I remember the house felt weird. Empty. Turned out Dad had come home early to take her to lunch. They never came back."

The room is silent in the wake of the young man's grief. Celia looks up at Felipe, asking him with her eyes if he'll release the boy so she can hold him properly. She isn't surprised when her master shakes his head. Felipe is much too cautious about Celia's safety. What could this boy do to her really? She rolls her eyes, but her lips betray how charmed she is by her enigmatic lover. She's come to respect his logic over the years; he's a hell of a chess player.

"Celia, give the boy more water," Felipe voices gently.

Kid drinks the few sips offered to him and barely manages to keep himself from begging for more. "Why are you being nice to me?"

10. Kid

Kid finds Celia's presence oddly comforting, considering she's made no move to free him. His mother had been a loving woman, always hugging and kissing him. He'd loved it as a boy, hated it as a teen, and aches for it as a young man. He shifts closer to Celia.

His uncle Tiny had never been one for heart-to-heart talks, even if it was his own brother, Kid's father, who'd died.

Felipe laughs. "I'm not being nice, boy. I'm deciding what to do with you. The men who brought you have gone for a while. Your female companion has been found responsible, and her fate is out of my hands. That leaves me with you."

Kid shakes within Celia's arms. "If you already know I didn't do it, why did you ask me?"

"I had to know if they'd broken you."

"Is Nancy dead?" He doesn't want her to be dead. No matter what Nancy has done, she's paid. They've *all* fucking paid.

"She's alive. Though, like you, she probably wishes for death. The two of you have angered very dangerous men."

"Caleb, you mean." Kid's stomach cramps a little more. He hasn't seen or heard Caleb since being taken hostage. He has no interest in a reunion. He recalls with too much clarity their introduction.

Felipe sighs. "Yes, Caleb is *a* dangerous man. Unfortunately, he is not the only man upset by this situation. Tell me—because I sense something else is in play—why do you suspect Caleb reacted so…passionately? Could it be he has affection for his captive? I'm curious."

Kid recoils sharply away from Felipe's stroking thumb. The affection is unwarranted and reminds Kid of the taste of his own tears and Tiny's blood. Caleb and

Felipe are obviously cast from the same mold, perverts who like touching his mouth.

Felipe chuckles and pats Kid's bruised cheek, not ungently. "I'm an extraordinarily curious man…*Kid.*"

"She ran away from him," Kid manages to say. "Tiny said we were helping her escape."

"For a price," Felipe accuses.

***

Tiny walks to the door and makes sure it's locked before he addresses the club. "I hope you assholes are ready to make some serious money. That girl is worth a hundred grand once we get her to Chihuahua."

Hog is the first to speak. "What the fuck, Tiny? You go out for a beer last night and come back with some girl? Who the hell is she?" he asks the last in an angry whisper.

Kid keeps his mouth shut, as usual, while the other guys murmur in agreement with Hog. Kid is just as curious as everyone else, but Tiny is his only real family, so he tries not to piss the man off. Maybe the girl just needs a ride and is willing to pay a lot to get there. Kid shakes off his stupidity. No one pays a hundred grand for a damn ride.

"What are you?" Tiny admonishes. "You a bunch of pussies now? I took a ride over to the bar after I hooked up last night, and the bartender let me drink. So, he's bringing in crates and I'm sitting there, having a beer and minding my own damn business, when this half-naked girl runs in screaming for us to lock the door." Tiny instantly commands attention. "Her and the bartender are shouting back and forth. Apparently, the girl's being chased by some guy named Caleb, who's been keeping her locked up for weeks. Dude! She didn't even know she was in Mexico! How fucked is that?!"

Hog sits up straight and lifts his hand. "Wait, wait, wait. You're telling me that girl has people looking for her? And you want to take her with us to pick up our shit? Are you crazy, man? Have you lost your goddamn mind?!"

"I'm not done!" *Tiny shouts and Hog falls silent.* "The bartender freaks and leaves me there with this girl. She won't stop crying and asking me to take her to the cops, which is stupid, because the guy who took her could easily bribe the cops. I'm in the middle of telling her this, when the fucking guy starts pounding on the door. Girl hides under the bar and I cover her with the crates the bartender brought in. Then, bang! The door gets busted in."

"Fuck!" *exclaims Joker.* "Man! I wish I'da been there!"

"Right?" *Tiny laughs. He starts pacing, engrossed in his story.* "So in walks this pretty-boy—no offense, Kid."

"Fuck you." *Kid rolls his eyes and pretends—like always— not to be offended. The guys frequently like to remind him of his 'cock-sucking lips' and 'bitch-looking' face. It's been old for a long time.*

Tiny laughs and keeps talking. "He's already blown through the door, so I know the damn shotgun he's carrying is loaded. I play it cool and pour myself a beer." *He grins.* "Right away, he asks about the girl, and I tell him I ain't seen her. We go through this whole thing, sizing up each other's peckers, and then I pull my gun out. This fucking guy…he doesn't even flinch. He tells me he's willing to pay if I bring him the girl—he's staying in that old plantation. And then he leaves, just like that. He even shows me his back, like he didn't give a shit if I shot him."

"Man! What? Serious?" *Joker is enjoying himself immensely.* "What are we waitin' on? Let's just give her back, let him pay us off. I ain't ready to head out yet."

Tiny scoffs. "Yeah right, that guy would just as soon kill us after we gave up the girl. Witnesses, stupid. Besides, I already made us a deal. Her friend's willing to meet us in Chihuahua and pay. I told her no cops or we'd kill her. All we have to do is get there."

Tiny opens his arms wide and beams. "A hundred thousand fuckin' dollars, guys. That's double our usual take."

"We ain't in the kidnapping business, Tiny!" Hog stands abruptly, nose-to-nose with Tiny. "Cut that fucking girl loose and let's get out of here before anyone comes lookin'."

***

11. Felipe

"I didn't care about the money," Kid sobs. "Uncle Mike…Tiny." The boy appears at a loss for words and Felipe supposes he can't really blame him. The young man has been through quite an ordeal the past couple days. "I couldn't leave Tiny. He's…he *was* my family," Kid continues solemnly. "We were just supposed to do what we always do: run a few kilos of cocaine and pot across the border. Once a month, like clockwork. No one ever gets hurt. No one ever…no one…and then…"

"Hmm," is all Felipe plans to say on the subject, but then he adds, "You didn't know with whom you were dealing."

Kid shakes his head. He *still* doesn't know. "Please, just tell me…are you going to kill us? Me? Nancy?" He's completely despondent. Felipe finds it…rather adorable—not the young man's suffering so much, but that he has no guile. He must have been a terrible criminal.

"You haven't answered my question yet. What is it you want most? Death? Revenge? Your freedom?" Felipe's tone is much too jovial for what he's asking. It earns him a baleful look from Celia. He shrugs.

The young man considers Felipe's question for a long while before he takes several deep breaths and shudders out a reply. "I can't have what I want most," he whispers, still unable to open his eyes. "There's no one left to love me." When Celia shifts him, he readily takes comfort in her awkward embrace.

"Devoted *and* sentimental," Felipe muses. "There may be hope for you yet." Felipe paces; his shoes make shuffling sounds along the concrete floor.

"He's perfect for us, Felipe. Don't you think?" Celia continues to place butterfly kisses on the boy's head. Felipe enjoys seeing her this way. Saliva gathers in his mouth as he gives her an infinitesimal nod.

"You're quite handsome under all those bruises, aren't you, boy?"

12. Kid

Kid hasn't thought much about his nudity, but he does after Felipe's comment. It's hardly the first time someone has mentioned Kid's appearance. As far back as he can remember, he's been complimented on his near-platinum blond hair and striking blue eyes. Kid has his father's strong build, but he's looked like his mama from day one. The girls have always gone crazy for him—and a few men too. He remembers his dad poking fun at him over his pouty lips and inability to grow more than sparse facial hair.

Kid also remembers his father's warnings about men who would take advantage. More than a few times, some asshole has tried to grab his dick in a men's room and had to be reminded what the word *no* means. Regardless, he's never thought of his looks as a bad thing, not until he found himself helpless. He forces himself to remain languid in Celia's embrace as he begins to cry, in the hopes it will solve his problems—no matter what his dad taught him.

13. Felipe

"The way I see it," Felipe begins, "your options are limited. I can't let you go, but I have no use for a hostage." Kid sucks in a breath and huddles closer to Celia as Felipe continues. "You've trifled with some serious people, boy. They're the kind who buy and sell fine-looking creatures...like Kitten, whom your friends have ruined, and occasionally, blond-haired and blue-eyed boys...like *you*."

"Please," Kid pleads, "just—"

"However! Let me finish, boy. Occasionally, masters find it difficult to part with their slaves." Felipe cannot resist a pointed look toward Celia. "So difficult, in fact, they keep them for themselves and spoil them rotten." Celia's tinkling laughter brings a broad smile to Felipe's lips.

"Am I spoiled, Master? Perhaps you should take me in hand and teach me humility?" Celia bites her bottom lip and drags her gaze possessively over Felipe's form.

Minx! Felipe is just about to respond in kind, when Kid interjects.

"What does that mean?" Kid asks. "I don't understand what you're saying!"

"It *means*...Celia has asked me to consider you," Felipe snaps. "Don't interrupt. I have no time in my life for insolent pets. No matter how attractive they are. *Comprendes?*"

Kid nods.

"Good. Your options are these: find it within yourself to submit to Celia *and* to me…or I'll leave you to Caleb and his sadistic master. They'll most likely kill you…or worse." He kneels beside Kid, purposely crowding him against Celia and the beam at his back. "You see? I am not a nice man, boy, but I *can* be fair. I'll spare your life, and in return, you'll surrender it to me as Celia did many years ago." He pulls away and stands.

14. Celia

Celia is aware she shouldn't like this as much as she does, but there are some pleasures she simply won't deny herself. The young man in her arms is quaking, muscles locked up tight. She reaches for his exposed penis and cups him firmly.

"What are you doing?" Kid rears away from Celia's neck. "Not there!" He presses his knees together and struggles in his bonds. It's useless, and all he's done is trap Celia's hand between his legs. Her fingers continue to stroke him, slowly, gently, and as enticingly as she is capable, which—in her estimation—is guaranteed to rouse this beautiful boy in her arms.

"Shhh, *no llores pobrecito*. Don't cry." She drops her voice to a husky whisper and nuzzles the boy's ear with the tip of her nose. *"There's no need to be afraid. I have you now. Give yourself to me, sweet boy. Let me take care of you."* Kid's muscles gently relax as he is lulled by her tender words, but his passion remains uninspired, even after several minutes.

"You're not doing what Celia wants," Felipe teases. "Is she treating you too kindly?" On silent cue, Celia applies greater pressure.

"Stop!" Kid hisses. "Please...I can't." He thrashes, and Celia immediately reassures Felipe of her safety. Her master is not easily convinced, but neither is he easily deterred.

"Celia, the boy would rather take his chances with the others." Felipe speaks as though he hasn't a care in the world save for his own amusement. Celia knows his ploy.

She resumes her previous less abrasive touches, and presses her lips to Kid's ear. "Come with me. Come for me." She's mildly irritated by her limited English. It forces her to use clipped phrases that undermine her intelligence.

"I can't," he says lowly, but his head finds its way back onto Celia's shoulder. "Hurts...they hurt me."

"Focus on the pleasure and the pain goes away," Felipe suggests. *"Celia, I think he may need more encouragement than your tender affections can achieve. Perhaps it would be best to simply move things along? He's going to acquiesce; he has no choice. It's cruel to keep him in suspense, don't you think?"* He smiles and Celia will swear she can see the devil in his eyes.

"By all means, Master, school me in the ways of seducing shy young men." She mirrors his Cheshire grin, eyes locked on his as he crouches in front of their quarry.

Kid yelps when Felipe's strong, masculine hands pull his knees up and apart. "What are you—" Celia's arm curves around his head to cover his mouth. Kid heeds the warning and cuts himself off from further protest.

"Do not be escared," she says in her accented English. She knows the idea of being fucked petrifies the boy, perhaps disgusts him, but she is convinced he only fears and abhors what he has never allowed himself to experience. Felipe is a skilled lover. She can attest to his prowess.

Celia grins as Kid buries his nose in her neck and deposits a series of pleading kisses against her sensitive flesh. She rewards him with encouraging sighs and light touches for several minutes before she extricates herself to stand. "Open your eyes," she says firmly; she and Felipe are in this together.

15. Kid

Kid forces himself to obey as much as he's able. With his head craned back and his eyes half-open, he stares up into the faces of his new captors. He'd been expecting…well, he wasn't sure who he'd been expecting, but not the two looming over him. Felipe looks to be in his late thirties or early forties. Kid raises a brow, soaking in the fact Felipe is wearing a flamingo-pink suit. He's going to get fucked by an old guy in a pink suit. Fucked by a man with dark, salt-and-pepper hair and a five o'clock shadow that would take Kid a month to grow. Fucked. By a man! The floor is suddenly very interesting.

Felipe laughs. "Don't worry. I'm not offended. I'm a lot more handsome if you like men. You obviously do not." He smiles when the younger man meets his stare and gently shakes his head. "Yes, I know, but let us not forget about Celia."

Celia is…well…Kid's embarrassed he couldn't get hard for her…and that he cried. A lot. She's wearing nothing but a tiny pink tube dress, and raven hair is pinned away from her face to reveal dark eyes rimmed with darker lashes, a delicately pointed nose, and full red lips. Kid unwittingly calls to mind the kiss they shared and her possessive touch upon his flesh. Shame is swift on the heels of the unwanted pleasure that trills though him. The humiliation lasts long enough for him to remember she's the kind of sick bitch to jerk a guy off against his will. Kid surmises she's older than him by five to seven years. He gauges her height at a measly five feet. Felipe was smart not to let her come alone; Kid could easily overpower her, even in his weakened state, and is just panicked enough to have tried.

"Like what you see?" Felipe tilts his head toward Celia.

Kid averts his eyes. "I guess," he murmurs. He isn't going to admit to another man, a lunatic, that he thinks his girlfriend—or *slave*—is ridiculously hot.

Felipe pats Kid on the head, chuckling. "Smart boy." Both men focus on a simpering Celia. Felipe tsks; it's meant to be an admonishment, but only fond amusement shines through. "Celia doesn't like your answer. If I were you, I'd answer her properly." Felipe clarifies, "Yes, Celia, or no, Celia." He winks before he stands.

Celia wastes no time in pulling her slight pink dress down toward her waist to expose her small breasts and raspberry-colored nipples. She tugs on the modest peaks until they tighten. "You like me?" she asks.

Kid can neither deny his desire nor abandon his instincts. The nicer the carrot, the more brutal the stick—and Celia is one hell of a carrot. He licks his lips, wishing they weren't so dry. He looks at Felipe before he answers, cautious. "Yes, Celia?" He relaxes some when they smile.

"Good boy," Celia says, as though mimicking Felipe. She moves to take a step forward. Felipe puts his arm out to stop her.

Felipe addresses Kid with a deadly seriousness. "Hurt her, and I will take my time gutting you." Kid shuts his eyes. *There's the stick.* Instinct bids him to gather his body closer, hide his soft parts, and play dead, but he knows it won't do any good. He only has two options: Obey or die. Instead, he forces himself to breathe slowly and nod. He is meek as a scolded child under Felipe's scrutiny.

"Felipe!" Celia reprimands. Mischief twists one side of her mouth into a half-smile before she straddles Kid's hips and sits in the cradle of his spread knees. Her bare pussy rests against Kid's barely thickening cock. "Please?"

Felipe kisses her upturned lips. "I know, my dear. I promised."

16. Celia

Celia thanks Felipe in Spanish before she refocuses her attention on Kid. The boy beneath her is terrified, but pliant, willing to do anything if Celia will set him free from his suffering. She rocks her hips back and forth, tiny thrusts that rub her clit against his cock. She ignores his aggrieved whimpers as her slight weight reignites his pain. She only cares his cock is finally getting hard. Still, she keeps her tempo steady and predictable so Kid can brace slightly when she pushes back against his balls.

At length, Kid finally catches Celia's rhythm. His whimpers drift toward reluctant moans and his hips timidly thrust. Beneath his moist lashes and swollen lids, Celia can see dilated pupils. No doubt dehydrated, hungry, and delirious, Kid is finally getting some relief from his suffering.

"Mmmph," he cries. His timid thrusts get a little more pronounced. He's doing it. He's spreading like a whore for his kidnappers. Celia groans filthy and low in his ear. She owns him.

"She likes that, boy," Felipe whispers intimately. "She likes your little boy cock getting hard for her. *"Verdad que sí, Celia?"*

"Sí, Felipe," Celia hisses and grinds down on Kid's cock. All he does is moan.

Felipe's low, throaty words continue. "Fuck a little harder, boy. Show her how hard your rosy little cock can get. It is not often she gets to play with such pretty toys.

Is he handsome, Celia?"

"Yes, Felipe," she whimpers. "Pretty boy."

17. Kid

Kid is being used, molested, but his body only appreciates the way he's floating above his pain. Yes, his cock is hot and pulsing, but it's the rush of mind-numbing pleasure he gets with every thrust that rules him. He can't help himself; he's a living, breathing mass of pure need. His cock surrenders precum in spite of his dehydration. Maybe they'll give him water. He thrusts more confidently. Maybe they'll feed him. He whimpers, pushes his cock through the slickness gushing from Celia's sopping pussy. Maybe she'll let him sleep in her bed. Maybe she'll slide his dick inside and let him come. His balls tighten at the thought and another series of whines escapes him.

Celia leans forward. Her breath quickens and her chest is slightly tacky with burgeoning sweat as it makes contact with the side of Kid's face. Her hard nipples drag against his neck. Kid is too far gone to contemplate sucking on Celia's tits. He is too out of his mind to acknowledge she is sucking Felipe's dick as he stands to the right and behind his shoulder. If there's drool dribbling on him as Celia gags on Felipe's cock, he ignores it. He feels no pain.

Celia says things Kid doesn't comprehend or take notice of until a masculine hand lands in his hair. "She wants to know if you like this." Felipe grins and tugs Celia's face toward his cock.

Kid shouldn't have looked up. Felipe's cock is big, bigger than Kid's for sure, and there's just no way it won't hurt. He's not going to take it well, probably cry like a little bitch the whole time. "Oh, God," he cries. "Please stop."

Celia whines around Felipe's thick, uncircumcised flesh. "Shh," Felipe comforts. He strokes both their heads. "Don't be scared, boy. I wouldn't defile your pussy in such squalor. I can wait. Apologize to Celia."

"I'm sorry, Celia," Kid says without hesitation. He's not going to say anything about his 'pussy'; his scarlet blush is comment enough. With the threat of rape removed for the time being, he's too relieved to fight. He's close to the end, and oblivion waits if he can just get there. He keeps his hooded gaze on Celia sucking Felipe's cock like a porn star, unable to resist thrusting his own hips as Felipe tells him again what a good boy he is for making Celia happy.

All the praise is screwing with his head. Kid can barely hold himself together. The urge to come is overwhelming. Thoughts of his own cooperation humiliate him, excite him, destroy and remake him. Felipe tilts his face up and Kid stares up into calculating green eyes. He doesn't look away, even after Felipe removes his hand from the younger man's head.

"So good," Felipe groans, eyes fixed on Kid. Abruptly, he pulls away from Celia's mouth and moves behind her. He pushes Celia forward until she and Kid are resting one another's heads on each other's shoulders. He reclaims his hold in Kid's hair, pushes into Celia, and comes.

Shock assails Kid, lust quick on its heels. Above him, Celia cries out as Felipe thrusts into her ass. She rolls her hips rough and fast, milking Felipe's cock. Seconds later, semen trickles onto Kid's throbbing erection and his sore balls tighten sharply. Pain, not pleasure, ripples through him with every shot of come pushed onto his own stomach.

Kid passes out before shame can find him.

***

18. Celia

Celia watches Reynaldo's back intently as he carries Kid's limp, unconscious body up the stairs. The young man's long limbs dangle and sway with each step, but their head of security is careful not to let any part of the boy bang against a wall.

She's deeply pleased by the latest events. Behind her, Felipe runs a hand up and down her leg as they walk up. *"Well? What do you think of him? I think he's wonderful—beautiful, open, achingly sweet, and did you notice how your orgasm affected him—it was his trigger."*

She can hear the smile in Felipe's voice when he replies, *"I noticed. I also took note of your reaction to him—you're smitten. Admit it."*

Celia giggles. *"Perhaps a little, but no more than you. You're not the only one with eyes."* She looks over her shoulder to deliver a cheeky wink before returning her attention to Kid's bouncing feet and shapely legs. A smirk tugs at the corner of her mouth.

"You recognize my preferences better than anyone, my dear. How can I resist?

It works in our favor Rafiq is occupied with the woman. Our only obstacle to keeping him will be Caleb, and I'm fairly certain his imposition in our lives will provide me the leverage needed to convince him the boy should remain with us. He will *want the boy punished though; you know that."*

Celia's brows furrow and her mouth twists in disgust. *"Yes, we'll make it a spectacle of humiliation. Though, if Caleb is anything akin to Rafiq, I'm not sure I'll be able to stomach his presence. That poor girl he's kidnapped…I cannot wait for the day we are no longer beholden to men like them; they disgust me."* She halts her steps and turns when she no longer hears her master walking up behind her.

Felipe is serious. *"Do I still disgust you, Celia? I'm no different than they are."*

Celia sighs wistfully. She takes two steps down to her master and wraps her arms about his neck. *"Please don't say such things. They hurt me."*

"I will ask the same of you." Felipe speaks tenderly.

"Yes, master." She kisses her lover's strong, firm, and domineering lips—so different from the boy's. She is a slave to these lips.

They walk the rest of the way to Celia's room in companionable silence, fingers interlaced.

19. Kid

Fear is a constant emotion in the wake of Kid's capture. Released from the dungeon and dragged upstairs into a lavish mansion complete with chandeliers and Persian rugs, Kid has no illusions about an end to his torture. Every moment is tense. Every touch, nefarious.

He isn't allowed to wash himself; Celia scrubs him down and shaves him from nose to balls while Felipe watches menacingly. The older man smirks when Celia demands Kid spread his ass cheeks for her to remove the sparse blond hair around his asshole. Kid doesn't dare to breathe as he complies. He fights back tears as Felipe compliments his 'shy, pink hole' and 'virgin pussy'.

Kid is tempted to grab Celia and hold her under water until Felipe agrees to let him go, but he knows he'd never get away, and truthfully…Celia is kind of nice—still a perverted cunt—but genuinely concerned with Kid's well-being. She's very gentle with him, careful not to nick or cut, always sure to show him what she's going to do next. She cleans his scrapes, kisses his bruises, and offers reassuring words in a language Kid only ambiguously understands.

Afterward, he is wrapped in a black silk robe that smells faintly of cologne and fed a familiar meal of seasoned steak—precut—rice, and beans. Kid chews slowly, the way Felipe asks, because he doesn't want stomach cramps. He's rewarded with more praise and three Vicodin. He even manages a mumbled 'thank you' to his gracious captor.

Washed, fed, and medicated, Kid is in no condition to refuse an invitation to lie in a frilly and enormous bed. He can hear Felipe speaking to him—Kid's body is made for pleasure—he must obey—continue to be a good boy and show off his pretty parts—he belongs to Felipe and Celia—obey—obey—or suffer. Kid allows his mind to descend into his nightmares, more comforted by them than his reality.

***

Celia speaks. Felipe translates: "Put him on his knees and lock his wrists to his ankles." There's applause.

Kid digs his heels into the floor. He's blindfolded, gagged, and surrounded by strangers. He panics, struggles against the men forcing him to submit, incensed by the laughter of his sadistic audience. A low warning is whispered into his ear, "The master said to remind you what can happen if you're not a good boy."

Hesitant knees find their mark and Kid allows himself to be bound. Whatever's going to play out in the next few minutes, Kid would rather believe it can't be as horrible as the alternative. *Please, God, don't let them pass me around like a party favor. Pleasepleasepleasepleaseplease.*

Delicate fingers tuck his hair behind his ears. The faint scent of apples enters the intimate space between their two bodies. "Shh, *pobrecito*. I'm good to you." Kid barely has time to digest the situation before Celia fists his overgrown hair and snaps his head back.

"Fuck!" Kid lets out a muffled bark. He wasn't expecting pain, not from Celia. His shock makes him realize how naïve he truly is and he chides himself. No one here is his friend.

"Does it hurt, slave?" she mocks. Soft laughter ripples through the room.

Kid is silent. Behind his back, his fists clench and his arms strain against his restraints. Celia pulls harder, wrenching his head back in such a way to completely expose his throat. "Yes…Celia," he manages around the gag. All at once, he wants to die, he wants to murder everyone in the room, and he wants to weep in Celia's arms. The only thing Kid can hear is his own heartbeat and frightened breathing. He can't see Celia, but he can feel her in the empty space between his vulnerable body and her comforting softness. He's desperate to close the gap and escape their avid spectators.

"Very good, slave." Felipe's voice is scarcely above a whisper when he translates Celia's words. She releases Kid's hair and he audibly sighs in relief. She strokes his gold strands for a few seconds before she unbuckles Kid's gag. Her audience sighs approvingly as they listen to Kid pull in ragged, humid breaths. Celia wipes away the drool on his lips.

Kid feels unhurried, seductive fingers caress his face, neck, and shoulders. Her touch is quickly becoming familiar. He appreciates the way she coaxes him toward genuine desire; he feels less violated when he wants it at least a little. His pride stings, but he prefers this method of torture to the others. Celia's scent blooms over a wave of aroused heat Kid swears he can feel against his naked chest. He inhales swiftly before he can prevent himself. An image of her tight, raspberry-colored nipples perched on small breasts invades his pitch black sight. If he leans closer, he can take one in his mouth. She pulls away. He narrowly avoids falling on his face leaning after.

Kid is distressed without Celia to keep him engaged. He listens intently to every sound. There are whispers and stifled giggles. He startles when the room erupts in laughter. "Damn it, Felipe," says a man in a thick Texas drawl. "You are a lucky bastard. Go on, honey—you teach that boy a lesson."

Kid licks sweat off his upper lip. He whispers his plea just as he feels her presence. "Celia..." *Help me.* Her hand briefly cups his cheek and he is immediately distressed by the combination of her gentle touch and harsh tone.

He hears Felipe translate: "Put your face on the ground and lift your ass in the air." Kid doesn't move to obey. He's paralyzed. The crowd hisses in disapproval.

"No?" inquires Celia.

"Please," Kid says. He hardly recognizes the sound of his suddenly prepubescent voice. If he ever thought he was a badass, it was a fantasy. If he is anything, it's cursed. "I've had enough. No more."

"Enough? I've barely started," simpers Celia. "And of course…" Kid waits with bated breath. "You forgot to say: Please, *Celia*." Kid feels a blow across his chest before Felipe can finish translating. It stings like fire! He groans and bites hard into his lip as he attempts to rub his chest against his knees by doubling over.

Kid is struck across the back before he can pull himself back up. His only warning before the next blow is the keen swish that signals Celia's arm coming down. He lowers himself. He braces. His groan is loud and open-mouthed. "Will you obey me?" she asks insistently.

"Yes, Celia," Kid spits through gritted teeth. The crowd applauds.

"Prove it," Celia purrs. "Lift your ass."

Kid would swear he has ice in his lungs. It was one thing to fall apart in the basement, another to offer up his body to Celia and her twisted boyfriend, who would gut him if he said no…but *this?* One of his buttocks is prodded pointedly and he teeters on his knees before finally achieving the position Celia demands. Kid lacks the will or presence of mind to disobey. Since his parents' death, he's been follower, a relaxed, agreeable person. He has relied upon his malleable nature to gain friendship, love, and companionship. He relies upon it now to gain his next breath.

Celia drags long leather strands across the bare expanse of Kid's flesh. Naked and tightly bound, he has no choice but to accept what is about to happen to him. His breathing hastens, sounds ragged, and each breath moves his entire body. The tips of the flogger kiss his balls. He hisses, writhing against the carpet. "Do you like that, slave?"

"No, Celia."

Another tap. "That's not polite. Shall I hit you harder? Like a man?" Hushed squeals of delight and muted chuckles erupt around them.

"No! No, Celia. I'm sorry. I'm sorry," Kid pleads. He sobs into the carpet after a series of fierce blows strike him across his ass. He counts them, unexpectedly convinced they are his penance.

One: I'm sorry I didn't try to save you, Uncle Tiny.
Two: I was scared and
Three: I don't want to die.
Four: Please help me.
Five: I'm sorry.

"How was that, slave? Hard enough?"

"Yes, Celia," he mumbles brokenly. He wipes his face on the carpet, slowly and repeatedly. The gesture is less to remove tears, spit, and snot from his face, and more to appease some baser need. A distressed sound bubbles out of him when gentle fingers drift along his reddened skin.

"You're doing so well, slave. Just a little more and I'll reward you," Celia croons.

"Th—thank you, Celia." Kid can hardly breathe, let alone speak, but he struggles to get the words out anyway. His humiliation is momentarily usurped by his keen need to keep Celia happy, if for no other reason than his distaste for pain. Though, the strange desire to return to Celia's room and her bed also exists. He wants to be held again. He keeps the thought close once his penance resumes.

Six: This is my life now.
Seven: It's just as well.

Eight: I wasn't ever gonna—
Nine: do much of anything.
Ten: Dad knew it.
Eleven: Tiny knew it.
Twelve: Maybe Mama knew it too.
DON'T EVER THINK LIKE THAT!
Thirteen?
Fourteen?
Abruptly, Celia stops.

Kid is jostled into a different position. As blood rushes away from his head, he feels his consciousness fade in and out until he has to be held in place by heavy hands. Celia's breath tickles his ear before she speaks. "Open for me." Leather brushes the inside of one thigh and then the other, and Kid parts his knees as wide as he can with his wrists and ankles shackled behind him. He doesn't have the opportunity to think on his obedience before he is distracted by the serpentine quality of Celia's voice as she whispers hungrily into the shell of his ear.

"Can you feel him watching us? So jealous of your youth...and yet willing to let me taste you." Celia trails the flogger leisurely across Kid's bare cock and balls in long, slippery strokes. Little by little, Kid's cock begins to fill, growing hard despite the resurgence of his shame. Despite an audience. Despite his fear. He doesn't understand Celia's words so much as his body responds to their evident intent.

Possessive fingers take up residence between Kid's thighs. The first sensation he can process is a ripple of relaxation as his mind signals his body to focus on a caress along the freshly-shaved skin of his sac; he had been anticipating an attack. His hips loosen and the muscled globes of his ass return to their resting position. His balls descend from their hiding place; his shoulders drop as well. He draws in hiccupped breaths and shivers as he exhales. "Ohhh," he groans, in agony, in acute ecstasy. The second sensation is uninhibited pleasure. His body throbs and he rolls his hips to be that much closer to Celia as she envelops him. "Yeah," he sighs into the skin above her breasts. "Right here…stay right here…please, Celia," he whimpers, trying to move even closer. His body innately sways, part exhaustion, part comfort mechanism; he hums; he murmurs. "I'm so sorry…"

"Good boy," Celia says lowly. The words are meant only for Kid and they affect him all the more for it. He groans deep and low—a debauched and wanton plea. At last, he registers his yearning.

Desire rips through him voraciously. Celia smells decadent, like syrupy fruit and musky arousal. His tongue darts out experimentally and savors a hint of salt that only whets his appetite. Visions of his lips latched onto one of her little nipples as he fingers her pussy lash him with want! He rattles his restraints. "Please," he growls. His cosseted body thrusts in time to a litany of accented, lyrical praise: *Beautiful boy…so good…all for me.* There is something depraved happening; his cock is engorged in equal proportion to his childlike elation at Celia's words. Kid marvels at the way his pain simmers as his pleasure mounts. Sensations, both painful and forcefully pleasurable, radiate outward through his body. Celia's gentle hands and tenderly spoken whispers are his entire world, a world where his mind is both separate from his body and completely attuned to its needs. He wants to stay forever. Forward and back, his hips work to keep his rigid flesh in Celia's hands.

"Greedy slave," Celia whispers into his ear. She brushes her nipples against Kid's chest. "Would you like to suck me?"

Kid nods. *Yes! Anythinganythinganything.* "Yes, Celia." Celia removes her hands from his cock to tease his mouth with a pebbled nipple and a cruelly spoken order to *suck*. Kid opens his mouth. He moans, loud and unabashed. His cock jerks in midair. His pain forgotten, he latches on and suckles Celia in long, ravenous pulls that have her gasping and pulling his mouth closer.

"Yes!" Celia cries, "Suck harder."

Kid obliges, drunk on sensations he can't name. He only pulls his mouth away to breathe or switch breasts. There is a loud pop as Celia pulls away. "No…wait." Kid stumbles and is caught and steadied on his knees by Felipe's surreptitious henchmen.

Celia returns before he descends into panic and places a hand on Kid's head to hold him steady. "Now, suck this."

Something *not Celia* nudges Kid's lips and taps his teeth. He rears back like a spooked horse, shaking his head in the universal sign for 'What the fuck are you doing?' and 'Stop it'. Celia doesn't bother to take his body language into account. She raises the flogger and strikes him across the chest with so much force there is a collective wince in the room.

"Suck it!" Celia repeats. Kid opens his mouth on a frustrated sob. There are entire years he has forgotten and there are days he knows he'll never forget; half of them have occurred in the last few days. The second he acknowledges he is on his knees in front of a room full of people, sucking a huge rubber cock, sporting a diamond-hard erection, and making little noises that sound somewhere between 'Please fuck my mouth harder' and 'Please, God, no more'—Kid's cock throbs and leaks a generous surge of slick.

"Yes," she chuckles, "you are good boy." Her small hand cups the back of his bowed head, and with the other, she hooks her thumb into his mouth beneath her cock. She strokes his tongue and pulls him closer.

Kid can't help but imagine what everyone else can see—a weeping boy with genderless features sucking a cock attached to a girl half his size. There is laughter every time he gags and Kid sobs around the cock in his mouth, but he is almost sure he's weeping for the wrong reasons. He's enjoying this—taking pleasure in his own suffering. How did it happen? Why is he fucking loving it, and hating it, and needing it?

By the time Celia gives the order to set him loose so he can fuck her, Kid doesn't give two goddamns about doing it on the carpet in front of a room full of strangers. Blindly, he reaches for her and tosses her to the ground with brutish force. He revels in her abandoned cries, in the way she spreads her legs and opens her arms to invite him close. She makes no attempts at all to stop or guide him. She gives him everything. Everything! And she's right—Kid *is* greedy. His hips tilt back, gauging. He thrusts forward into Celia's pussy. They both whimper as he pistons in and out of her slippery heat. He thrusts, and he thrusts, and he thrusts until his balls feel heavy and tight.

"Ah…ah…fuck…oh…mmm…gonna come…yeah, oh yeah…God!" He comes hard and long with his face buried in Celia's neck and his body holding her immobile in his desperation to fill her with his seed. Celia offers him words of encouragement that set his soul on fire. "Yeah," he pants wetly. "Immagoodboy…mmmgood…I'm…feel high."

Celia kisses his damp head and shields him as adequately possible.

20. Felipe

"You did very well tonight, boy." Felipe's thick fingers brush along Kid's lips. The boy snatches his head away and Felipe chuckles. "You don't like that, do you? I imagine such a pretty mouth has many admirers?"

"Fuck you," Kid replies hastily. The boy is blindfolded and shackled spread-eagle against the cold tile of Felipe's black playroom shower; his pale skin is stark in contrast.

Felipe wants this boy in every way imaginable. He finds himself charmed by his childlike petulance; he reminds him of Celia—without the cunning. "Language," Felipe tuts silkily, "such filth shouldn't come out of such a pretty mouth." Again, his fingers cannot resist skimming over the tremulous pout of Kid's sinful mouth. The boy sniffles and turns his face away. "Still don't like it, I see," Felipe rumbles. "Celia is correct; you reek of corruptible innocence. It is…tempting." He leans closer to Kid's shackled body, presses his nose into the soft flesh at the center of Kid's ribcage, and inhales slowly. "Or perhaps I only smell my Celia on you. If I go lower, I suspect I'll smell her womanly juices on your little boy cock." He revels in the mingled scent of feminine arousal and the boy's own acrid semen scent. His mouth is watering.

Kid's muscles tremble beneath Felipe. The boy whimpers and presses himself against the wall at his back as though it might give way. He has to recognize the futility of his attempts at modesty, but Felipe appreciates his new lover's beguiling efforts. A predator prefers his prey to run. Felipe's tongue darts out to gather a taste of skin. He groans low and fierce. *Ambrosia.*

"F-F-Felipe?" His beautiful boy pleads, "Please…stop. I don't want this."

Felipe's tone is pure amusement. "You don't want this?" He stands with his hands on the younger man's hips. Kid is an inch or two taller; he can likely feel Felipe's breath just under his chin. "You agreed to belong to me."

"To Celia," Kid whispers. Felipe's fingers dig into his hips.

"And to whom does *she* belong?" There is a thinly veiled threat in the words. He presses bruises into the tender skin over the bones of Kid's youthful pelvis. It doesn't take Felipe long to hear the answer he is looking for and he relents. "That's right, you ungrateful boy, she belongs to me, and so do you—*if*—I desire it." *And oh! He does.* "Or, if you prefer, I can always return you to Caleb; his girl isn't much use at the moment."

"No! Please, no. I belong to you. Do whatever the hell you want, but please keep that goddamn psycho away from me!" Kid thrashes in his restraints. "He killed Tiny! He! He…"

"Shhh, shhhh." Felipe moves quickly, surprised by Kid's genuine panic; he aligns himself along Kid's splayed body and closes the distance between them to keep the younger man sandwiched tightly between him and the shower wall. "Of course you belong to me, boy, of course." His words are mawkish, but effective. Kid's breathing slows, his muscles relax, and after a few minutes, he surreptitiously nods his head.

"Just do it already." Kid shudders. "I won't fight; I can't." His breath catches several times before he says the words that both shock Felipe and make his cock leap painfully in his trousers. "But…just…don't be a dick about it. I've never..." He can't even say it without bursting into tears. Kid's penis remains flaccid between their lower bellies.

Felipe's voice, once he's capable of speech, is dangerously deep and lustily rough. "Language, boy, last warning." The older man grinds his erection against Kid's cleanly shaven genitals. "And just what is it you've never done that has you flushing so beautifully for me?" He breathes in through his nose. "You smell delicious, like Celia's unappeasable pussy." He whispers in Kid's ear, "I wonder if your pussy will be as good as hers."

"I don't have a pussy," Kid whines.

"No?" Felipe coos. "Then what's this?" He circles the tight pucker of Kid's anus with one spit-slick finger. His boy's pussy is small.

"It's my asshole," he sobs. "You know it's my asshole. Stop it!" He devolves into wails of despair. "I didn't do anything! Please...I didn't do it."

Felipe decides to remove the blindfold, unsurprised when the boy asks him not to—it's his only shield against his own debasement. Kid keeps his eyes determinedly closed. "Open your eyes, pretty boy; let me see." A moment later: "Right now." When Kid remains disobedient: "Do it, or I'll open you without lubrication." Felipe's finger continues its gentle twirl around Kid's rim.

Seemingly calling upon every scrap of self-preservation, Kid timidly opens his eyes. Felipe gives him time to adjust to the bright light in the room reflecting off the onyx tile. The boy doesn't dare to acknowledge Felipe, just keeps his eyes on the drain in the floor.

Felipe's arousal reaches new heights when confronted by the younger man's timid responses to having his tight little asshole gently worked. The boy's warm breath puffs across Felipe's cheek with every muted gasp and subsequent exhale. Felipe gently prods his rim and Kid shuts his eyes tight and whimpers. Felipe's head falls forward so he can whisper things in a litany of Spanglish against his young lover's neck. *"Open your eyes. I know, sweet boy*...so tight...*Celia*...clever girl...*we're going to have so much fun with you."* Felipe is starting to sweat and his finger gets bolder with every pass over the boy's hairless pucker.

"Lube!" Kid bellows. "You promised." Fat, salty tears and watery snot trickle toward his quivering mouth. He keeps his eyes to the left of Felipe and focused on the floor; they close briefly as Felipe's palm cups his moist cheek and turns his head to face him. Felipe stares into vibrant blue eyes.

"Let me set your mind at ease, beautiful boy. One day soon, you'll beg me to come inside you." He taps his finger on Kid's hole. "Until then, you'll appease me with your submission or I'll rid myself of the nuisance you present. Am I understood?" Kid's affirmative reply is softly spoken between them. "Good. Now...what is this?"

Kid's face is a study in misery. He shatters like glass and his voice sounds just as broken. "My pussy."

"And whom does this pussy belong to, boy?"

"To you," Kid submits.

"All together, boy. I like to hear it." He slides his finger over Kid's perineum and around his hole in a never-ending circuit.

"Please," Kid begins before the look on Felipe's face gives him pause and he gives himself over fully. "My pussy belongs to you, Felipe."

"And are you going to let me fuck your pussy one day, boy?" His question is met with silence, and then...

"Yes." It's barely audible.

"Say it."

"I'm going to let you fuck my pussy." Kid appears surprised by his own words.

"Yes," Felipe whispers with a hint of triumph, "we understand each other now." He unzips his pants with his free hand while the other carries on its previous attentions. Laughter rumbles out of him as the younger man startles and his boy pussy instinctively shrinks away from his formerly—and deliciously subconscious—accepted touch. "There's just one more thing left to do, and then you may have a reward."

"What are you gonna do?" Kid mewls. He is every bit his nineteen years—all man on the outside, still a boy in his heart.

Felipe is struck by the young man's innocence. He was satisfied before, but for the first time has no doubts he had nothing to do with the attempted rape or beating of Caleb's slave. Kid may have been associated with a group of drug-running outlaws, but the boy is no man of action. Not like Felipe, or Rafiq, or Caleb—if they are wolves, Kid is a wounded lamb. A delicate feeling takes up residence in his chest and quickly travels south. He will show mercy, he decides. "Celia has marked you. I will as well." He can't resist rubbing his hard cock against Kid's flaccid one. The younger man's gasps and whimpers are sure to become an aural fixation. "Be a good boy and keep your eyes open. I like looking at you. Don't be so sad." Felipe pants. "You're mine now, my prize, and I'll take care of you." All of this foreplay has him in quite a state. Celia is magnificent with the boy. She plays both the simpering imp and the predatory succubus with sublime elegance. Seeing them together was an exercise in restraint. "We will cherish you as the lovely boy you truly are. Celia will act as your new mother, I will be your new father, and you shall be the obedient son we can never have."

21. Kid

"You're sick!" Kid sniffles. The older man is masturbating on him—circling his asshole—and he has the audacity to implicate himself as Kid's father? "My dad never!" Kid is tempted to tell Felipe to go fuck himself, but he doesn't. There is no purpose in tempting Felipe toward doing more with his finger than teasing. He can do this. He can get through this ordeal and... *And what? I have nowhere to go and I'm too scared to die. I'm a coward, a fucking pussy.* He opens his eyes again and lets Felipe take his fill of his despair.

22. Felipe

Felipe chuckles. "Of course not. There's nothing incestuous about what we'll do with you, boy. I'm simply offering what you clearly lack—a mother figure to hold you, and a father to guide you—approval they can no longer give you—discipline you never learned."

"You...crazy! You can't just treat me like some kid; I'm grown." Kid is a weeping mess, but he's careful not to curse.

"Not to me!" Felipe groans and plants his face in the crook of Kid's neck as he comes in thick spurts over the boys genitals. He smells Celia. Pressed along the younger man's displayed body, he indulges in the mingled scents of semen, vagina, and Kid's fear-tinged sweat. He moans, and much to the relief of his new bedmate, slides his finger away from the boy's pussy. He leans away to look at his new ward; he's exquisite. Celia knows his preferences remarkably well. Kid is flushed all over with embarrassment. His sobs echo around the room. Still, the boy keeps his eyes on Felipe. Belatedly, he gathers up some of his fluids from Kid's stomach and brings them up to the boy's mouth. "Show me what a good boy you're going to be for me."

Kid recoils with a violated shudder. "Come on, man." He outright screams when the force of Felipe's open palm sends his face to one side.

"That is not how a good boy replies!" Felipe reprimands, even as he uses the same hand to soothe the red mark on Kid's cheek. "Don't you want to be my good boy?" he asks more softly and sighs when the only response is an elongated cry. He's not made of stone. "You're going to be a willful little boy, I can already tell." Felipe infuses as much tenderness as he can manage toward Kid into his words. He strokes the boy's hair until he has his breathing under better control. "There," he croons, "there's my boy. He's so good. So brave. Deep breaths…that's it. Be brave for me now. Be the good boy I know you are." A wave of haughty satisfaction crashes over him and he laments his inability to get hard again so soon as the boy slows his breaths and lets his eyes gently glaze over. He scoops up more come.

23. Kid

Kid doesn't know why he opens his mouth to Felipe's fingers; the act seems natural. The taste faintly registers. He hears only praise and feels only comfort. Kid wants more gentle touches, more worshipful words spoken softly into his ear…more…more…more. *I can be brave. I can be good. Don't leave me. I'll be good. I'll be good. I'll be good.* The older man has him enthralled.

24. Felipe

"Such a sweet boy." Felipe kisses the boy's sweaty head and runs his come-coated fingers though his mussed strands. He is completely unsurprised by the way Kid leans into the possessive touches. It's obvious what the younger man has been missing and Felipe intends to give it to him. And if Felipe takes what he craves from him in return, well, he supposes it's only as it should be. "You were perfect, Kid. I couldn't have asked for a better boy." Kid whimpers. "Would you like your reward?"

"Yes, Felipe," Kid says in monotone.

"Very well, after I bathe you, I will take you to Celia and you may sleep with her in her bed. I know she's eager to apologize for thrashing you in front of our guests…but it was the only way to convince Caleb and Rafiq to place your punishment in our hands. Forgive her, won't you?"

Kid sniffles, "Yes, Felipe." He adds, "Thank you," unexpectedly.

"You're very welcome."

25. Celia

"Celia," Kid whispers in the dark. "I know you don't speak English so good, but do you understand it?" He curls himself, nude and still damp from his shower, closer to Celia.

"Little bit," she replies gently. *"I grasp more than Felipe suspects, but less than he would like. Do you understand me?"*

Kid huffs sarcastically, "All I got was 'Felipe suspects' and 'do you understand me'. Is that close?"

"Little bit," she replies. She grins into the boy's hair and keeps stroking him. Her young lover suffers so superbly. Just the thought of cracking him open and forcing him to spill all his pain into her waiting lap has her achingly wet. Felipe is such a good master. He gives her only the best offerings…and she only accepts the ones of benefit to her master in equal measure.

26. Kid

Celia rolls her hips and Kid shudders. Sex is the last thing he wants and the only thing he can think about. He's been rescued, molested, beaten, and maybe raped— he's not sure if a dildo in his mouth counts. It's been a hell of a fucking day, and all he wants is for this striking, cruel goddess to hold him like a fucking baby and rock him to sleep. "I'm scared," he says lowly. "I know men aren't s'pose to say stuff like that, but…every time I close my eyes, I see blood." He's fairly certain Celia doesn't follow what he's saying, though, the way her arms pull him closer so she can kiss his temple suggests she recognizes what he needs. "My whole life is over, like I never existed. I'm gonna die here and no one is even gonna care."

27. Celia

The boy is sobbing again, and no matter how sadistic Celia can be, she cannot abide him thinking he's worthless. She and Felipe will humiliate the boy in every conceivable fashion, but they will never let him think he is unwanted or unworthy. He is precious. "We care," she says fervidly and tips the boy's chin back so she can stare into those pleading blue eyes. "Felipe and me, we are good to you. You our good boy." She bites his lips playfully. "So pretty."

He tries to resist it, but he smiles, if a bit warily. He speaks, but his words are indecipherable to Celia. "We are wordist people you meet? What is *wordist?*" Celia's nose is wrinkled as though the word tastes bad in her mouth.

Kid genuinely laughs; the sound of it pleases Celia. "*Weirdest*…it means strange. You and Felipe…you're…strange."

She grins. *"I'll delight in showing you how peculiar your new bed partners are."*

"I heard monster? Cowboy, and bed."

Celia laughs throatily. "We tich eashother how to spek. *Felipe will help us in the beginning. He would never pass up the opportunity to play out his student-teacher fantasies.*"

"Yeah, okay, that sounds good. What'd you say about Felipe?"

The young man in Celia's bed is refreshing. Things had been stale lately, but the past few days have brought much-needed excitement to her and Felipe's tiny world of two. Between Kid, Caleb, and Kitten, her master never wants for entertainment, and she knows he is watching her and this boy from his secret room. She drags her bewildered pet on top of her and wraps her limbs around him; her eyes are directed toward Felipe's 'hidden' camera. *"Come here, sweet boy, let me make you feel better."* She cups Kid's rounded behind and smiles when she discovers tiny hairs standing on end and gooseflesh.

Kid holds himself perfectly still until he is firmly gripped and pulled forward by his flank. He braces his body, unwilling to crush her with his weight; Celia takes advantage of the opportunity to guide Kid's shy erection into her. Kid groans.

"Good boy," Celia says affectionately. "You are not scared." She kicks the sheet down to the foot of the bed with her legs, exposing the scene. She urges Kid to thrust with her hands and feet on his ass. She feels the exact moment of his acquiescence; he melts into her with a whimper and makes short, slow, and ardent thrusts into her.

Celia opens for her lover, folds her knees, and bends nearly in half to allow him to lick the inside of her mouth and stay buried to the hilt. His desperation is her aphrodisiac; she clenches her muscles. *"He feels so good inside me,"* she mewls. The boy's rhythm falters and picks up speed. *"He...mmm...thinks the deeper he can...yes, baby boy, right there...bury himself...the longer he can hide."*

28. Kid

Kid isn't listening to a word Celia is saying. He likes the way she sounds in his ear though—pliant, encouraging, and aching for it. Hours ago, she was raping his mouth with a rubber dick, and now she's wet, flushed, and open beneath him. Touch. Connection. Comfort. Celia is all of them. Kid lifts her torso so he can hook his arms under her and grip her shoulders. He wants them pressed together like they were never meant to be apart. *They're all gone. I'm all alone.* He thrusts as slowly as he can, unwilling to let his fear enter. "Celia," he pants and searches for her mouth. He comes before he's willing and stays inside until he slips out wetly.

29. Celia

Celia's tummy flutters. She takes every drop her precious boy has to give, swallowing him deep into her barren womb. She runs her fingernails lightly over Kid to feel him shiver. She smiles morosely into the camera. *"I didn't come. Tomorrow we'll have to teach him manners."* She sighs. *"Goodnight, master."*

30. Kid

The first several days are jarring.

Every morning, Kid wakes to the realization he is not in his bed. Soon after, he recalls he's being held in a house full of people who want to either murder or molest him. His heart always races afterward, and he tries to go back to sleep, only to find all he can see is his uncle's disembodied head and his empty eyes staring at him. From the moment he is awake, he knows the day is going to test him. He invariably huddles closer to Celia, who speaks soft, unintelligible words to him. They give him hope in spite of his inability to translate them. He has no family, no friends, and no say over his fate, but he clings to the hope he is somehow not alone in the world. He matters. To someone. He has to.

His afternoons are a torturous affair. Kid never knows what devious thing Felipe or Celia have planned, but he knows one or both of them has something to contribute to his 'training'. Once or twice, Kid has made the mistake of thinking Celia is the lesser evil between the two, only to learn they are interchangeable in all the ways that matter. Felipe uses skilled intimidation to bend Kid toward his will; Celia uses expert seduction to bring him to his knees—they both know how to break him. Every afternoon, he abandons his pride and surrenders his body, and little by little, he can feel himself giving up something far more important.

Evening heralds the worst part of Kid's day—when Felipe insists on bathing Kid before bed. It's always just the two of them—and Felipe's stern-looking watchdog Reynaldo—in the vast but intimate space of Celia's bathroom. Felipe praises him for his obedience throughout the day and gently criticizes his hesitancies. The ritual of forced familiarity between them causes Kid great distress for a variety of reasons. He experiences twinges of guilt for his supposed failures, made more poignant after Felipe's fervent praise.

Kid shouldn't want to please Felipe, or Celia for that matter, and he doesn't…it's just…he hates *displeasing* them so much more. He turns his head to the side when Felipe starts to rub off on him. He grows increasingly worried over the few times his own penis has stirred; it happens most when Felipe's warm seed spatters over Kid's cock. The younger man accepts Felipe's presented fingers, because he knows he is expected to do so without question. He is both glad and wary of the fact Felipe's taste is becoming less abhorrent with each offering.

Bedtime is his favorite time of day, because he gets to lie down next to Celia and be normal. She calls him Kid and he calls her Celia. He fucks her and she lets him do it however he wants—he opts for missionary with lots of kissing. No mistress. No slave. Nothing kinky. Kid has good reason to be angry with Celia and to avoid her; she is no different from her master. She is equally twisted in her desires, loves to see him cry and beg and come all over himself as Felipe plays voyeur, but Kid can't bring himself to resist her sinister allure. There is the illusion of safety inherent in her femininity; he feels less threatened and insecure.

Kid rolls onto his back, sweaty and sated, knowing that another trial waits in the morning. He shuts his eyes to avoid it.

***

There is something happening, some plot, or betrayal—Kid isn't stupid—he knows. Felipe's had a lot of visitors lately; mean looking guys who like to talk in hushed tones. Kid is usually sent away soon after the conversations begin, but a few times he's been ignored and allowed to stay. He sort of wishes he hadn't been.

Kid doesn't want to consider the possibility more violence is on its way. He's just started to believe he might be... *okay*, not happy, or perfect, or not metaphorically shitting his pants every now and again... but—things are... okay. Kid has never been so well-fed in his life. A week ago, he tried something called creamy pappardelle; it had bacon in it, and these crunchy things called leeks. Delicious.

Celia is teaching him Spanish. Kid is teaching her English in return, but she isn't as good a student. Kid believes it's because he doesn't get to spank her every time she gets the alphabet sounds wrong. He learns shockingly fast by comparison; his ass is more ruddy than red lately.

True, Felipe and Celia run him ragged on a daily basis, and they're always asking him to do embarrassing crap like dress up in ridiculous costumes—two weeks ago, Celia outfitted him as a pony and rode him around the mansion dressed as a Lady. Kid had been relieved to know only the skeleton house staff and Celia's security detail could witness his shame, as Caleb and Kitten were rarely seen outside the typical guest areas and Felipe was out on an errand for a few days. But then, while still in costume, Celia commanded him to mount her 'like a stallion' on Felipe's sixteen person dining table and Kid suddenly lost his distaste for wearing ears and a tail. He came fast and hard.

And *yes,* Kid and Felipe still have their nightly ritual, and Kid still resists the older man's advances. Although, he's given up on trying not to get hard when Felipe starts rubbing his pants against his bare cock and circling the rim of his asshole so gently Kid wants to scream; the worst nights are after he's been kept on edge all day.

So things aren't ideal—they're better than they've been in a long time. Kid is worried it's all about to change again. He hears the name Rafiq a lot. *Rafiq needs to show more respect. Rafiq cannot hold the shipments. If Rafiq wants more product he has to buy it from us, not Caesar and his idiot brother. Something will have to be done about Rafiq.*

The Night Devils are—were—small time, only a step or two above the street dealers. Felipe works on a global scale. He's most likely supplied Kid the weed for every joint he's ever rolled. Men like Felipe tend to die bloody. If Felipe is in danger, they all are.

31. Celia

Her boy is fitful. Celia can feel him tossing and turning, huffing and puffing; she can practically hear him thinking.

"Celia," he finally speaks into the darkness, "are you awake?"

"No. Sleeping," she mumbles. "You sleep too." She half-heartedly emphasizes her request with a kick to Kid's shin. She doesn't bother to stifle her giggle as Kid hisses in pain.

"Punk-ass, can't believe you kicked me," he says without heat. Celia turns and they share a look before saying in unison, "Language, boy!" in a parody of Felipe's scandalized tone.

Celia sighs. "I wish he come home. I don't like when he's away. If he meet another woman and she steal his heart?" She doesn't typically entertain those types of thoughts, but every now and again, she wonders if she's still enough for her master—considering.

Kid scrunches his face. "What? Trust me, that would never happen. Felipe worships the ground you walk on. No way he'd give you up."

She smirks. It's nice to share these moments with someone. Kid is very sweet. *"You sound certain of whatever it is you're saying."*

"You didn't get that?"

"Enough." She switches to English and continues, "Felipe is complicated man. He say he is happy, but...he always want *more*. He is...how do you say? *Oportunista.*"

"An opportunist."

"Yes. He would not...leave us, but he maybe..." Celia's eyes mist with tears. *"It's possible that one day he will find someone to give him what neither of us ever can."*

"What are you talking about? You give him everything. I have no idea why he keeps me around, other than to have someone to tease."

Celia laughs softly. She reaches into the sheets and tugs her young lover closer by his hand. His skin was much rougher a month ago; though, he still has grease stains beneath his fingernails. One day she will beg Felipe to let her go for a motorcycle ride with Kid. She cannot remember a time she's gone anywhere without an armed detail. Her father was an overbearing asshole, and Felipe worries too much. Kid worries too much too. "He like you, protect you, keep you. Do not worry."

32. Kid

Kid rolls his eyes but leaves it at that, because Celia's words make him want to squirm in a way that feels less and less like disgust, and more like…butterflies in his stomach, or some girly crap like that. He'd be lying if he didn't admit to growing more curious about what his life could be like if he gave himself over to the life Celia and Felipe are offering.

"How did you, with Felipe, end up?" Kid stumbles through his Spanish. He can understand it much better than he can speak it, but his fluency is on the rise, much to his master and mistress' delight.

33. Celia

Celia's smile takes on a devilish quality. *"He took me as a trophy after he destroyed my father. It put fear into the hearts of anyone who would dare oppose him. Fuck with Felipe Villanueva and he will murder you in your home and steal your daughter for his concubine. Quite effective."*

"Why does that make you smile? He killed your father! He took you prisoner!" Kid says caustically and full of reproach. Celia finds his anger ignorant and incendiary. She won't tolerate it.

"You are prisoner too!" Celia snaps in English. *"Felipe takes what he believes he is owed and nothing more. For years I begged him to kill my bastard of a father. I offered myself to him as payment; he refused. But little did I know he would deliver me vengeance one day and demand I make good on my promise.*

"He had my father's empire, but it wasn't enough and I've been with him ever since. Do not presume to know our master. He has his own honor and we are lucky to have inspired his affections." She glares at Kid, the insolent little brat.

Kid's indignation wilts under the heat of Celia's death stare. "I didn't really get all that, but I get that Felipe sort of did you a favor. My bad; I don't know the guy that well, except for the fact he's always trying to fuck me."

Celia laughs. "He is not."

Kid balks. "Uh, yeah, he fucking is. He's always talking about…well, you're there—cheering him on." The boy sneers. "You always take his side—always—and it's not fair. I never have a say."

Kid pouts and Celia's stomach can't help but flutter. He's utterly naïve; it makes her long for her own long-lost innocence. Felipe is devout and steadfast in his seduction, and she knows in her heart that one day she will surrender to his will. He will own her, body, mind, and soul. She will keep fighting against it, but one day…
"Felipe save your life. He feel he own it. But your spirit, you have to give him. He wants you to give to him. *He'll seduce your body until it craves him. He'll worship you until you feel the intense desire to be worthy of such devotion. You can only think*

of his happiness and the way it shines on you, makes you feel weak and invincible all at once." She wistfully looks toward the hidden camera in her room. She knows Felipe will watch the playback. He always does.

"Yeah," Kid says, "I get it. If he was going to do it, he would've by now. That right?" His face tells Celia he isn't finished speaking; he seems exasperated. "I just…why's he gotta try and make me ask for it. It's bullshit. I'm the prisoner. Why doesn't he just take what he *obviously* wants and lemme be?"

Celia knows well the turmoil Kid suffers; she's felt it in one way or another for several years. It is her deepest hope that one day she and Felipe will move on from the hardships of the past toward a fulfilling future. Felipe's intentions in gifting her with Kid as a companion are either a stepping stone toward that future, or a white flag.

"Would you like to hear a secret?" Celia adjusts herself onto her back so she can stare toward the camera.

"I'm not gonna get my ass kicked for knowing, am I? 'Cause if so, I'd rather you didn't tell me."

Celia is charmed by Kid on a consistent basis. "You are silly." She takes a deep breath. Her smile slowly drops. "Felipe and me…we don't make sex."

Kid props himself up on one elbow; his shock and incredulity is painted all over his face. "That's bullshit. You had sex on top of me the first time I met you!" He apologizes quietly when Celia angrily clucks her tongue and shakes her head.

"Don't interrupt. I meant to say we don't…do it the natural way." She places a hand between her legs for emphasis.

"You don't let him fuck your pussy?" Kid looks doubtful and sputters on, "But that's crazy! You're his bitch." He hisses a breath and rubs at the sting across his cheek.

Celia pops her knuckles by making a fist and then shakes out her hand. "Language, slave, or I will tell master on you. I am not a bitch!" She crosses her arms under her breasts.

"No, Celia, not like that." Kid lowers himself to the mattress, holding his reddened cheek. *"You're not a bitch. A bitch is a girl—I mean—I—we—used to call girls that when they belonged to one of the guys. I'm sorry."* Kid stares up at her, contrite. "Please...don't tell Felipe."

"Okay," Celia huffs, "but you don't say anymore. I am a slave, but no one own me. I am not a bitch." She turns her back on Kid and stares into the darkness of the room. It's not often she allows her emotions to get the better of her, but Kid and his crass sincerity can be too much sometimes.

A single tentative finger touches Celia's back. "Celia?" When she doesn't rebuke him, Kid shifts closer, his palm delicately pressed against her spine. "Please, don't be mad at me. I didn't mean it like that."

Truthfully, Celia is not angry. She fears the pinprick behind her eyes that signal the onset of tears—real tears—the ones she no longer allows. She has often questioned her relationship with Felipe, the love she has for him...the lingering spite. She has been keeping a close watch on Kitten and her master Caleb since they arrived, and the similarities between their relationship and her own consume her as the weeks pass. She can see the seed of love sprouting, growing, and it makes her ache; *that*, coupled with her new slave's open heart, conspire to undo years of practiced contempt.

"My father was a powerful man." Her voice is firm, steady, and devoid of emotion. She cannot feel this anymore, to allow it would mean her father still lived. *"There was nothing he could not do and no one he could not have.*

His power was absolute. He took my mother from her family when she was only fourteen. She died giving birth to me." Celia keeps her eyes firmly on the wall at the other side of the room, but she allows her young lover to nestle in close behind her. Kid craves affection like she once craved freedom. She does not deny him if she can help it, and right at this moment, their needs coincide.

"He kept me instead of sending me to the orphanage. I think he even loved me in his own way; he doted on me. I had the best tutors, wore the finest dresses; I had my own servants. But my father's attentions came at a steep price.

"I grew up beautiful…like my mother, he said, the first time he took me. I was twelve, and he was not gentle with me."

"Celia…" Kid pulls her into his body with a despondent sound. "*No*," he says, like he can erase the past by simply willing it. "I'm so sorry," he whispers.

An old pain ripples through Celia. Her lover is genuine and kind…sincere. He is nothing like her and Felipe, who trust no one and place their pride above even each other. She swallows thickly, and moments later, goes numb. "No sorry. It was long time ago. *Do not pity me—it's for the weak. I'm only telling you so you understand your place."*

"Yes, Celia," Kid replies carefully.

"Felipe worked for my father back then; first as my bodyguard, and then many other things as the years passed. Felipe saw how things were. He was not blind to my suffering at the hands of my father. He helped me get rid of the evidence of my first abortion, and the second. He watched over me during the weeks after I turned sixteen and learned I could never have children.

"He watched as I grew up cruel. I liked to whip my servants. I slept with my father's friends and his enemies just to provoke my father into killing them. They saw. They all saw and they did nothing. Felipe saw too, and I hated him most of all, because I knew he pitied me, but also that he desired me. It made me sick.

"I tried to seduce him many times over the years. Felipe never touched me. He used to say it would be like kissing a venomous snake. I had my father beat him bloody for saying such things to me. Afterward, I insisted he kiss me and beg my forgiveness. He smiled at me—the insolent man—smiled at me! He barely escaped with his life.

"Two years later, on the evening of my 20th birthday celebration, Felipe raided my father's villa. His men executed my father's security team, his guests, even the few servants who had come to our aid." She chuckles. *"He saved my father and me for last. I thought he would simply kill us. Instead, he asked how I would like my father murdered. I thought it was so romantic; I suppose I still do."*

Kid shivers. "You're really scary sometimes, Celia. I don't like it when you say things like that. You're not like them, not a killer, no matter how tough you try to be. You've got a good heart; I can tell." He speaks the words softly.

"You are a very sweet boy, Kid. Do you like being our slave?" She touches her index finger to his lips in a predatory fashion, satisfied with Kid's angry blush. Imagine—a blond baby chick making friends with a sly fox; the boy *should* be embarrassed.

"Whatever," he grouses. "So what happened? He killed your pops and the two of you rode off into the sunset together?"

Celia's amused smile slides into something hard. *"No, sweet boy, nothing so simple. You see, by the time I was twenty I was formidable, and thirsty for my father's blood. I cut off his manhood and fed it to him as he bled out. Felipe knew he couldn't have me as an enemy. I offered Felipe information he needed to take over as the head of my father's organization in exchange for my freedom. However, Felipe did not need my help and he had his own aims for my future. He was convinced there was a strategic advantage to keeping his former rival's daughter; who would go up against such a madman?*

"Felipe's first order of business was to repay me for my treatment of him over the years. I won't go into the specifics, but he beat me, forced me to act as a servant to the staff that had served me all my life, and yes, he forced himself on me. I hated him most for that.

"But years passed, and Felipe...changed. He wanted more from me. He wanted my love and devotion, and he set about getting it. But...you see...he and I are the same. We do not forget those who wrong us, nor do we forgive. Felipe has sworn to never again force himself on me and I hold him to his promise. I sleep with other people, let them have me in any way I'm willing to allow, but not Felipe. Felipe is denied entrance to the center of me. It is his punishment, my way of letting him know my love can only be given, never taken. It's been nearly five years and he's never tried." Celia feels a lump in her throat and pushes against it with her fingertips to smooth it away.

"There are days I feel myself surrendering in the face of Felipe's steadfast devotion. To my knowledge, he has never taken another female lover, never felt her warm, wet, womanly flesh wrapped around him. He accepts only what I offer and the occasional young men who catch his eye. On the surface, he does it all for me, but I know it for the battle of wills it is. I want him to beg me. I want him on his knees! But some days...I just want him. He's winning, Kid. He very nearly has what no man has ever had...my soul.

"He knows it too. That's why you're here—your youth, your innocence, your capacity for forgiveness—you're everything we've lost and all we hope to regain. I was never young, never innocent, but you remind me it exists; you remind us both. Through you, we have a chance to nurture and love, an opportunity for Felipe to treat his lover as he should have treated me in the beginning, and for me to have someone to care for without feeling weak." She kisses Kid's

soft lips, charmed by the slight scrape of patchy stubble on his upper lip and chin.

"So," he says and clears his throat, "is that why he's so obsessed with my *boy pussy*?" He grins cheekily until Celia returns it.

"You have no idea what I'm saying, do you?" She laughs heartily and kisses Kid all over his ridiculous face.

"I got most of it," he chuckles. "I'm just saying...maybe if you gave it up, he wouldn't keep trying to stick it in me. Couldn't you like...help a guy out?"

They laugh for several minutes before Kid's laughter begins to die. He rests his head on Celia's chest with a sigh and places her hand in his hair. He isn't sly at all with his demands; she strokes him the way he likes.

"You guys are fucked up." He sounds sad. "Seriously."

Celia kisses his head. "No one hurt you. You our good boy."

"Yeah," Kid says. His breaths are slow, but Celia can feel the force of his heartbeat along her side. "Okay."

34. Kid

Kid is shackled to the wall and waiting for Felipe, just as he is every evening. Today has been a particularly taxing day. Celia is apparently in a mood about something. She's been sullen and irritable toward Felipe. Her ire, in turn, has made Felipe more sadistic than usual. Kid has been ceaselessly tormented in the melee. He hasn't come all day, and he knows Felipe is coming to whisper filth in his ear while he touches Kid's *boy pussy* and jerks off on his nuts. Kid doesn't think he can take it.

He's already half hard thinking about it and his asshole feels…*weird. Empty.*

Felipe enters, Reynaldo respectfully behind. The master's foul mood is evident in the absence of his welcoming smile and the presence of a furrow between his thick black brows. He looks at Kid for several seconds before he relaxes his face. "Do not fret, beautiful boy. I am not inclined to vent my frustrations on you. At least, not with violence." He purposefully prods Kid's thickening erection. "Especially as it seems I am not the only frustrated party."

Kid can feel the heat of his embarrassment crawl up from his chest to paint him cherry red up to his cheeks. "You guys have been fucking with me all day. It's not…it's not because of *you*." He exhales sharply and forces himself to maintain eye contact.

35. Felipe

Felipe's formerly impenetrable ill-mood gives way to twisted amusement. "Language, boy. I've warned you what would happen." He chuckles heartily at the younger man's mortified gasp and penitent expression. *"Deberías ver tu cara!* Your face!" He cannot resist cradling the boys head in both hands and planting a hard kiss on his lips.

"Hey!" Kid protests and twists his face away from Felipe's tenacious grasp in an attempt to wipe away Felipe's kiss. "Stop that." He swipes his tongue over his lips.

The older man crowds his primed treat. He scents the young man from tense and muscled shoulder to soft and thin-skinned nape. He speaks softly into his ear. "I can't wait to taste you." He closes his eyes when he feels Kid shiver, and slides his linen-covered thigh under Kid's balls. "I'm going to savor every yielded ecstasy. I'm going to lick my essence out of your unrefined mouth until I can taste only your submission. I'm going to spread you open and spear your virgin pussy on my tongue until you cry out for my cock in you. I'm going to swallow your pink little cock and devour you."

36. Kid

Kid can feel the older man's knee between his cheeks, and the urge to grind his asshole down and fuck against Felipe's thigh is enough to force out an undignified groan. "No," he whispers close to Felipe's ear. *Don't make me give in yet. I'm not ready.*

37. Felipe

Pale hips flush with blood and the young man's cock plumps on top of Felipe's thigh. The older man artfully avoids giving his captive any accidental friction. The boy is easy game, a rabbit, far less complicated than Celia, who only pretends at being prey. "No," he repeats Kid's plea and meets his eyes. "Not until you desire it, not until you desire *me*." He strokes the boy's golden locks. "Until then, however, it is my duty to guide you into my service. I will do so by enforcing the rules I set. Your punishment for using vulgar language is one finger inside you…without lube." Nefarious grin in place, he strokes this thumb over the younger man's damp cheek.

Kid struggles uselessly in his bonds and stares daggers toward Felipe. The boy is full of impotent rage heaped on top of his own shame. "You can't!" he rages. "At least use lube, you dick!"

Felipe's amusement disappears like it never existed. He stares back at the younger man, matching and then surpassing his intensity until the boy looks away and shuts his eyes tight; a single tear slides down to the tip of his nose. Self-worth is a tenuous and fragile thing. Everyone must have it to be satisfied with their own existence, and yet, Felipe requires an equal amount of humility. What to do?

He tuts silkily. "You ask me for a favor and insult me in the same sentence? It is an interesting strategy, given that I am not accustomed to being called names to my face. It would be careless of me to allow you to think such behavior is rewarded."

"I'm sorry. It just came out." The younger man shrugs feebly.

Yes, Felipe muses, the boy's bearing has been battered the past week. All to the good though, he can sense how close his new charge is to succumbing to him and Celia. He can proceed with the punishment as prescribed and risk Kid's genuine disdain, or he can set out bait and let his little rabbit wander into the trap.

"Are you terribly unhappy here, boy? Do you wish Celia and I had left you in the cellar?" He asks the questions calmly, knowing they can be perceived as concern or a veiled threat. "Because believe it or not, I would rather you didn't hate me quite so much as you do. Am I so ugly?"

38. Kid

No, Kid's mind answers impulsively. He turns his face as far left as he can to avoid Felipe's warm, strong body still intimately invading Kid's personal space. "I don't know what you want with me," he grinds out. "It's not like I'm a threat to you. I could disappear and you wouldn't even notice." He's surprised by the pang exploding in his chest.

39. Felipe

Felipe's heart is the slightest bit affected by the younger man's self-defacing confession. The boy is perhaps more humble than Felipe previously gave him credit for. He recalls Kid refers to no one as his family or friend, and it gives rise to an unexpected paternal urge to comfort him. He buries his fingers in Kid's thick hair; it really is too long for a young man. "I would notice, boy…and I would be very put out. I am not interested in reluctant bed partners. It's true you are intrinsically here against your will, but it is my and Celia's hope that you will eventually become a part of our odd little family. If that is not a possibility…" he kisses the younger man's forehead tenderly, "perhaps you would be better off elsewhere."

Kid's eyes fill with tears, but his anger is evident. "Where?" he growls. "Where am I supposed to go? I don't have anything. I don't have *anyone!* I didn't do anything. I didn't kidnap a girl. It wasn't my idea to hold her prisoner. I didn't *ask* for any of this. And now I'm stuck having to choose between letting you stick a finger in my ass, or being packed off to God knows where. Gee, I wonder what the f—*heck* I'm gonna choose? Why don't you get it the hell over with so I can go to bed?"

Felipe takes hold of Kid's chin and enforces eye contact. "You're very ill-mannered, you know that? *I* did not bring you here; your choices are responsible. Still, I have kept you safe from those who would do you harm. I share my home with you. I share my woman with you. And all I get in return is your insolence and disdain. If I were you, I would weigh my opportunities with less flippancy."

40. Kid

Kid pauses and considers Felipe's words and decides they are overly pragmatic. Yes, in a way, Kid's own decisions have led him to his current predicament. However... "You can't really think that just because I didn't abandon my uncle I deserve this. You're taking advantage."

41. Felipe

Felipe raises his eyebrows, amused. "Perhaps." He takes a step back to admire his furious and despondent lover. He's tempted—oh, so very tempted—but his young charge is not yet ripe, and he wouldn't dream of forgoing the sweet taste of his willing submission. The older man sighs longingly, decided on a course of action, and undoes the black rubber cuff holding Kid's right wrist against the wall.

42. Kid

Kid doesn't trust Felipe for a second. He lowers his arm slowly and curls his fingers into his palm and against his bare leg. There are both questions and threats visible in his expressive blue eyes. Not sure what the older man is planning, yet unwilling to test his new master, he guardedly awaits instructions.

43. Felipe

"You may unbind yourself and bathe. When you are finished, Reynaldo will escort you to your own room." Before Kid can muddle through his shock and begin asking questions, he addresses Reynaldo. *"Watch him. Take him to the southeast corner, away from everyone. I'll leave something out for him on the bed—help him put it on before you retire. You're permitted to use force, but do not harm him unnecessarily. Make sure you lock the door from the outside. He is not to have any visitors other than myself."*

44. Kid

"Yes, sir." Reynaldo tips his head respectfully as the master departs. He fixes his hard stare on Kid. *"I have no idea what he sees in you, but you should have more respect."*

Kid removes his rubber restraints with one eye warily focused on Felipe's watchdog. The man, Reynaldo, always looks intimidating, despite being dressed as some sort of butler. Kid burns with shame in front of the shorter, bulkier, and serious Reynaldo when it occurs to him he has seen nearly everything Felipe or Celia have ever done to him. He's seen Kid cry, beg, and fuck. Did he see the reluctant craving on Kid's face as Felipe rubbed up against him? Most likely, he thinks. "Mind your own business," he mumbles and turns to start the water.

***

"Please, Celia," Kid pants. He shakes with need. He pulls on his tethers, secure in the knowledge they will hold him tight and keep him from touching. He only wishes they could keep his hips from thrusting. Above him, Celia's breasts, slick and shiny with sweat, bounce hypnotically. "Please let me come."

Eight days. It has taken eight days in a cock cage for Kid to crack wide open and beg. He'd thought it was stupid at first; he could handle not having sex. As long as he wore the cage, Felipe and Celia left him alone—no training, no pony rides, no nightly homo-erotic groping session. Kid just got to hang out in his own room and watch crazy Spanish soap operas all day. He was wrong. He needs to come. He needs to come right now. *Fuckfuckfuckfuckfuckcomecomecome.* "Oh, God, Celia…please. I can't hold it."

Kid's every would-be erection has been stifled for eight long, torturous days. The more he thought about not getting hard, the more his cock tried to fill in the cage. By day three, he had tried to rub off by cupping his nuts and gently squeezing his flaccid cock. He dribbled copious amounts of slick, but never came. Day four, Kid discovered how strong Reynaldo is when he tried to remove the cage and found himself summarily hogtied.

And then, last night…last night, for the first time in his life, Kid stuck a finger in his ass. Just to see what it felt like. Just because he'd heard guys have a spot there. He'd never wanted to try it before, because it seemed kind of gay, but then he figured it might make him come and he really needed to get rid of some of the pressure and it couldn't really be gay, because...it's his own finger. *Just the tip,* he joked to himself as he coated his fingers with spit and spread his legs to search out his asshole. It took a while to work his middle finger in deep. Kid moaned like a wanton slut for the better part of half an hour, but he still. Didn't. Come.

It's day eight. Day eight! And Kid's going to come today if he has to suck it out of his own dick and beg like a shameless slut if needed.

Celia rides them both hard, thrusting her ass against Felipe behind her, and her pussy down Kid's cock. Both men groan as their cocks struggle for purchase within Celia's body. The bed beats a staccato rhythm against the wall like a metronome keeping them in sync. Celia is insatiable. She will fuck for hours if Felipe allows her, and sometimes he does.

"Please!" Kid implores. He feels hot, suffocated, and overstimulated.

"No coming," Celia says. Sweat drips down her neck onto Kid's chest.

"Fuck!" Kid shouts angrily. He forces himself to change his rhythm to stave off the inevitable. He knows this game. Celia is setting him up for failure. He'll come without being given permission and Celia will punish him. Celia has seen to it by tying him down, sucking his dick, and riding him while Felipe fucks her in the ass. Even when Kid stops moving, he can feel Felipe rubbing him through Celia's tight, wet walls.

"Language, boy," Felipe grunts. "Celia isn't going to let you come." Felipe slows and swivels his hips in such a way that both Celia and Kid groan. "You're her distraction." He thrusts. "Without you..." Thrust. "She couldn't take me." Thrust. Thrust. Thrust.

Celia collapses on Kid's chest in a soggy heap. Her hair clings to his arm and shoulder. She pants hot, loud, and humid against his ear. "Ugh. Ugh. Ugh."

"I'm sorry, Celia," Kid says through clenched teeth. He won't come. No matter what.

Celia pushes herself up to grip Kid's jaw. Her nails dig into his chin. She trails her tongue over his lips until he opens to her kiss. She pulls back and groans. She stares into Kid's eyes. "If you come," she laughs at the pained sounds he makes, "I'll beg him to fuck you instead."

Kid's eyes widen. He thinks about how good it felt to fuck himself with one finger and how different it might be from taking Felipe's thick cock. His body heats up like mercury on a summer day, but he knows better than to show preference one way or the other. He might as well sit on Felipe's lap if he's going to succumb to that type of stupidity. It will happen one day, eventually, but he is in no hurry. Sharing Celia and knowing he cannot compete with Felipe is difficult enough, rolling over for him would be worse.

"Filthy little mouths, both of you. She never used to say things like that before you came, boy." Felipe smiles and keeps pounding his lovers into blissful submission as Celia asks Felipe's forgiveness. Felipe's hands cup Celia's breasts to pull her backward onto his chest, and Kid's pained moans roar to life. The older man shuts his eyes to better hear them, and Kid does nothing to keep them tempered. "Would you like that, boy? If I simply took what I wanted and deflowered your pussy? I bet you'd come without a hand on your little cock."

"Shit! I can't...stop...ohgod...*Felipe, please*," Kid sighs in defeat.

45. Felipe

Felipe punches his hips forward in shallow thrusts and nearly loses his control with every sharp clench of Celia's muscles and Kid's needy whimpers when their cocks grind and pulse together in her velvety grip.

"Can you feel me, boy? I can feel you. It makes me think about coming so you can feel every throb as I fill up our Celia's tight little ass. Would that make you lose it, baby boy? Make you come in her pussy so I can feel your cock against mine?"

"Ah, ah ah, ah…fuck…*goddamnitFelipe*. Pleeeeease!" Kid's hips stutter sharply. Felipe can feel the boy's balls tightening, ready to push out his load.

"Don't you dare!" Felipe says through clenched teeth.

46. Kid

Kid rebels against the vision of his own cock pushing against Felipe's as they flood Celia with come. Every thrust brings it back. He nearly screams when Celia hastily lifts off. Kid fixates on the sight of her bright pink lips quivering, and her vacuous little hole contracting around the ghost of his cock. Felipe's fingers fill her void, sliding inside to keep her coming. Kid can't tear his eyes away, not from Celia's juices sliding toward her asshole, not from Felipe's balls slamming against her, and not from the semen running back out.

Kid can no longer control himself. He curses them. He bucks wildly, pulling on the satin ropes that hold him spread out on the bed. His hard cock is red and leaking precum onto his stomach. "Please! Just touch my fucking dick. I'll come. Please. Please!"

47. Celia

Celia and Felipe laugh pitilessly as they fall to one side of the bed. Celia reaches out and lazily pinches one of Kid's nipples to make him hiss. "Shhh," she sings. "You know better than that."

"I'm sorry, Celia." Her young lover attempts to sound contrite, but his scowl gives him away. He's been starved for love and affection so long, and now that he receives it on such a regular basis, he's become a very greedy boy. Celia doesn't mind though; she adores her despoiled lover.

"Mmm," Celia purrs beneath Felipe's fingers. "What do you think, Felipe? Should we let him come?"

Felipe's laughter disrupts the bed. "He's nearly as spoiled as you are." He meets Kid's glare with a wink. "Besides, he's our slave. *He doesn't want this,*" he mocks. *"He only suffers our touch, mine especially. It's better if we give him respite from our lecherous activities."* He does nothing to disguise his self-righteous satisfaction toward Kid's leaking cock and pitiful, angry expression.

Celia shakes her head and scolds Felipe playfully with her eyes. *"As you say, master. But...shouldn't we at least give him a chance to come? He did hold himself back for me."*

"I did," Kid keens. His accent is improving.

48. Felipe

Felipe smiles and dips his fingers behind Celia; he brings them up shiny with their mingled fluids. He looks at Kid pointedly. "Open for me," he says seriously. The boy's wrists are tied, but his legs have been left free. He surpasses the older man's expectations when he plants his feet on the bed and lets his knees drop on either side of his long, gently muscled body. Any day before this one, the boy's face would be hot with degradation, but he cannot blush today. All of the blood in his young lover's body is throbbing in his cock, and Felipe knows a hard dick *has* no shame. "Good boy," he says gently and leans forward to whisper in his ear over Celia's shoulder, "but I meant your mouth."

49. Kid

Kid attempts to close his wantonly spread legs. Celia's smooth thigh pins his to the bed. They are both staring at him, and Kid can't help but feel like an ant under a magnifying glass. Felipe's smile is wicked, and Kid gasps when the older man slides his slimy fingers into Kid's mouth. They taste bitter with spunk and sweet with lube. He gags on Felipe's fingers, glad when they are withdrawn. He's about to remark on his displeasure when those same fingers, now glazed in his saliva, press against his exposed hole. Kid instinctively clenches, and he realizes he's been had as Felipe uses the opportunity to push a single fingertip past the first ring of muscle. Kid's eyes roll back into his head and he moans. "Ohhhhhhhhhhgodyeah."

50. Felipe

Felipe hisses hard through his teeth. Mary, Mother of God in heaven, Kid's moans would force a devout priest to sin. "Your pussy is so tight, boy. You're going to have to relax or I can't make it feel good."

"Feelsssgood right there," Kid slurs. "Mmph." Celia starts licking into his mouth and he sticks out his tongue so she can suck it. Felipe's cock tries to fill at the sight, but can't.

"Where is my finger, boy?"

"My pussy," Kid groans. "Felipe, jussdoit," he mumbles around Celia's invading tongue.

"You want more? Beg me." Felipe's voice is rough and husky with renewed lust.

"Please," Kid pleads with gusto.

"Please what, sweet boy? What do you want me to do?" Felipe croons.

"P-p-please…my pussy…I wanna come. Please." He lifts his free leg, opening himself. Felipe thrusts his thick finger all the way up the boy's ass. *"Ohgodohfuckohhhhh."*

"You won't come yet, will you?" Felipe growls.

"No," Kid squeaks.

"Tell me why." Felipe slides his finger in and out of the younger man's ass in a slow sawing motion that has Kid moving his sweaty hips up and down. He wants to lean forward and lick up the precum sliding down his blood red shaft, but Celia beats him to it—the greedy little minx.

"I'm your slave!" Kid shouts. His cock bounces gently against his own stomach with every wave of arousal.

"Yes. You are." Felipe slides a second finger into his young lover's snug hole.

51. Kid

Kid pants, swallows beyond the dryness in his mouth. Felipe's fingers feel like a claim, a brand being burned into him. He keeps his eyes fixed on his master and showcases his pleasure.

Celia's mouth closes over Kid's cock and Felipe pounds his hole so hard Kid's body is confused about what to do with the sensations coursing through him. Celia sucks once, twice, and Kid moans his pleasure to the ceiling as he unloads eight days' worth of come into her gluttonous mouth.

They all sleep in the same bed that night. Kid begrudgingly takes the middle.

***

52. Felipe/Kid

He grins impishly at the sight of Kid's bowed head as he takes a sip of wine. Lacking the ability to disguise his distress, the younger man has been staring into his lap for the past several minutes. He places his own bronze hand on Kid's blond head and takes a moment to appreciate the contrast. *"No tienes hambre, muchacho?"* he asks softly.

Kid blinks rapidly and shakes his head to clear his wayward thoughts. He looks up toward Felipe, perturbed by his master's genial expression. "I'll eat if you want me to, but no, I'm not very hungry." He gently leans into Felipe's hand.

The older man sighs and brings Kid's head down onto his thigh. Felipe is adept at sensing when his young lover needs reassurance. "Life has put you through a lot, hasn't it?" Kid nods, moves his knees closer to the legs of Felipe's chair. "Celia," he says and Kid's shoulders tense. Felipe moves his hand from Kid's hair onto his nape.

"She makes you happy...and you're worried she doesn't feel the same. If she did, she wouldn't take other lovers...is that what you're thinking, boy?" He massages the ridged muscles beneath his fingers.

"I'm just your slave."

"Hmm...true, I suppose. But you are not *just* anything, boy."

Unsure of his own intentions, Kid places a shaky hand on Felipe's knee. The older man has a gift for dragging all of Kid's insecurities out into the light where he can manipulate them as he pleases. Kid hates it; he loves it; he wants it to stop; he wants to beg for it to go on forever. Right now, the older man has him craving delicious praise. "What am I then?" he asks timidly.

"You're my beautiful boy." He puts his arm around the younger man and curls his body toward him until Kid crawls between Felipe's legs and wraps his arms around the older man's waist. Dark, strong fingers plow through corn silk hair. "You belong to me, to Celia—only you and no one else." Kid whimpers. "She adores her good boy...as do I." Felipe makes a hard fist; Kid whimpers louder. "You make such lovely noises, be it pain, pleasure—it doesn't matter. One cry and we want you. I go to bed at night dreaming of the day I'll bury myself inside you. Some nights, I can almost hear your debauched pleas in my ears." Felipe rolls his hips, scraping his covered erection across Kid's smoothly shaven cheek. Felipe likes to play in the gray area between what Kid thinks he can handle and what he can actually endure. A cock to the face through two layers of clothing is different than a naked erection.

Kid gasps. He shivers. "Fuck-toy," he whispers. "S'that all?" Two months ago, this would have freaked him right-the-hell-out, but a lot has happened in that span and he simply isn't the same person. He's a slave, a possession, a stripped-bare human being; he is his body, his desires, and his need—and nothing more.

"It doesn't have to be."

"What does that even mean?" Kid huffs.

Felipe chuckles. "If you see yourself as a slave, that is what you are. You could just as easily be our companion and confidant."

Kid's brows furrow. What would it mean to accept Felipe's words as truth? Could he really let this become his life, being a sex slave in a three-way relationship with a guy who can have people killed with a hand gesture and a woman who likes to dress him up like a pony, or a wrestler, or an Aztec? Does he prefer that scenario to the one where he's a nineteen-year-old high school drop out with no friends, family, money, or marketable skills? He closes his eyes and squeezes Felipe until his anxiety wanes. "I know why you let her sleep with other people."

"Do you?" Felipe keeps petting Kid. Dinner is only half-eaten, and despite the waste of a perfectly delicious game hen, he's happy to get this rare and intimate moment with Kid. Frankly, he's also put out by Celia's determined seduction of his new potential business partner. Felipe appreciates her commitment to him and their future, but these are dangerous times and he worries for her safety; Celia can be too brave. "Tell me, why do I allow her to sleep with other people?"

"She told me…that…um…she does it to get back at you…for…before."

Felipe laughs morosely. "Did she? Well, believe it or not, I was not always the refined man I am today. What else did she say?" Felipe already knows. He's seen the tapes.

"That she's waiting for you to stop her—that you never do."

"Why don't I stop her?"

"I don't know," Kid whispers.

"It's simple, boy," Felipe sighs. "I have no inclination to tame Celia's wild spirit. She wants to push me into becoming her father, wants me to control her by force, because she needs someone to rebel against. If there is anything I want to break her of, it's that. I want her to come to the realization she is mine of her own free will and that I am hers in equal measure. The further she wanders, the stronger our bond. Celia is mine; I simply don't make her admit it."

Kid scoffs. "Yeah, real *simple*. Sounds kinda stupid to me. You guys are so obvious. Why don't you say what you need to say and be done?" He looks up toward Felipe in time to see the other man throw his head back and laugh. Kid's chest unexpectedly expands with pride.

Felipe's laughter slowly melts away before he sets his glittering green eyes on Kid's upturned face. "I suppose…it keeps us young." He runs his thumb across the younger man's lip and is thoroughly pleased when his boy nips him instead of recoiling from the touch. "Please forgive us for passing messages through you, but anything coming from your lips is bound to sound best." They smile at one another for long seconds. "Go take your shower and meet me in my room. I'd like for you to sleep in the bed, but you may sleep on the floor if you like. I had Celia make it up for you before she retired for the evening."

Kid's face twists with uncertainty. "Take a shower…by myself? You never let me do that, 'cept for that one time and I had to wear that thing on my junk for eight days." He is *not* going to volunteer to wear that thing—it sucked, and no, thank you.

"Would you rather I bathe you?" Mischief is thick in his tone.

"Nope!" Kid scurries out from under the table and Felipe's splayed legs. Kid covers his ever-present erection with his hands and offers the older man a titillating view of his naked, pert backside as he walks toward the playroom showers at a brisk clip. He can hear Felipe's laughter in his ears as he goes. It makes him blush and grin.

53. Celia

Kid's hot length pushes at the back of her throat. She moans and sucks him deeper inside, choking herself on his engorged cock, reveling in the abandoned cries of her beautiful slave.

He holds tight to the ring dangling from the ceiling and keeps his bare feet on the floor through sheer force of will. He doesn't brace for the paddle. He lets his body absorb the dull thud—accept the pain Felipe doles out.

"*Gracias*, Felipe," Kid groans. "Oh, Celia. Please…ohgod…don't suck so hard. It hurts."

Celia pulls her mouth off Kid's cock with a loud pop and smiles with triumph at the long ropes of spit and slick clinging to the tip of her boy's flushed manhood. "You don't like it?" she pouts deviously. *"Do you want me to stop gagging on your dick, baby boy? I was hoping you'd come all in my mouth. You don't want to?"*

"I do! I do, Celia. I'm sorry. Please suck it again." He cries out in pain as Felipe's paddle comes crashing down on his backside.

"No. You upset me." She stands and wipes her chin, sure to suck her fingers clean. Kid's expression is pained, so sexy. *"If you want your little boy cock sucked, you'll have to ask Master. Maybe he'll let you come in* his *mouth."* Behind Kid's shoulder, Felipe grins and shakes his head before he brings the paddle crashing down on Kid's ass.

Felipe is fully dressed, shirt damp with sweat from exertion; Celia doesn't know which of her men is more handsome, more devout, and it thrills her to her soul she doesn't have to choose. Felipe pauses to press his body along Kid's back, making the boy hiss. "Would that please you—coming down your master's throat?"

"Please," Kid pleads.

Celia's body is tight with anticipation. *"Sí, por favor!"* Felipe isn't the only one who has been patiently waiting for Kid to finally say yes. Just the thought of the older man on his knees with Kid's dick fucking his face makes her pussy swell with need. Kid wants to say yes, she can see it in his eyes and the way his hips fuck the air. She doesn't resist the urge to spread her legs and finger her pussy in front of them.

Kid closes his eyes on a pained moan and dips his chin toward his chest. "Okay."

"No," Felipe says, "beg me, like a good little boy." Celia fingers herself faster as Felipe unbuckles his belt to unzip and fish out his thick, incredibly hard length to stroke the crack of Kid's ass.

Kid startles. "Not my ass!" He squirms, but continues to hold tight to the ring over his head all on his own. He swallows several times, panting. "Just...um...*suckmydickandletmecome*," he says in a rush. "Please?"

Felipe throws his head back and laughs. It makes Celia's heart feel like it's going to burst from joy. "Come on, boy. You can do a little better," Felipe croons.

Kid smiles, tries to hide it, and can't. "F-Felipe," he tries again, "will you please suck my cock? I...I want you to...taste it...swallow my come...the way you make me."

Celia has to put a hand on Kid's shoulder to brace her as she comes. Felipe's arm comes out from behind Kid to hold her close. She pushes her tongue into Kid's mouth and savors his submission until her orgasm passes and she can stand without assistance.

"Good boy," Felipe praises.

Celia takes up the paddle as Felipe circles Kid's dangling, stretched body and settles on the floor, his own cock in hand.

"Oh, God," Kid says. He shivers and Celia lets the paddle drive his hips forward, where Felipe is waiting to receive his reward for being a patient man.

Both men groan with pleasure the moment Kid's cock is sucked inside Felipe's mouth. Much to Celia's surprise, Kid's eyes are glued to Felipe's, watching his pink flesh disappear into the older man's willing, rapacious mouth. "Mmm...mmm...mmm." Kid fucks his master's mouth in time with his moans and Celia's paddle.

Celia beats her boy at an angle so she can watch the entire spectacle. Her own wetness runs down her naked thighs as she watches Felipe suck Kid's cock and stroke himself to orgasm. Her master looses a keening whimper of his own just before he paints Kid's left foot with come.

"I'm coming!" Kid warns and thrusts hard into Felipe's mouth, where his master is waiting to swallow every drop.

After several seconds, Felipe pulls away and says through panting breaths, "You're delicious, baby boy, just as I imagined." He kisses Kid's softening cock. "Let go."

Kid releases the ring and collapses into their waiting arms.

***

"Celia?" Kid inquires once they're alone in Celia's bed; she's already accustomed to his warm weight on her chest at night and hopes he'll never get his own room.

"Yes, Kid?"

"Will we ever be free?"

Celia hugs him tight. "I don't want to be free."

Kid nods. "You love him."

"I do." Celia kisses and strokes his hair just the way he likes.

Kid sighs. "He loves you too." Her young lover's fingers tap anxiously against her belly. He clears his throat. "Do you think you'll ever...love *me*?"

Celia tilts his chin up. She smiles, kisses his lips. "I do," she whispers. She watches his eyes as he processes this information; he wants to ask if she's implying she loves him already, or is open to loving him in the future. She witnesses the moment he loses his courage.

In the end, the boy only says, "Thank you."

Celia kisses him, savors him.

54. Kid/Felipe

The second to last thing Kid wants is to wake Felipe and stare into his pompous face as he realizes how unrested Kid is from sleeping alone and on the floor. Kid's distaste for having to suffer his master's smug satisfaction is second only to Kid's burgeoning proclivity to give in to the older man and willingly climb into the bed. Luckily, his need to make a decision is interrupted by the distinct sound of someone punching the security code into the door. *"Jefe,"* Reynaldo, Felipe's head of security, hisses into the darkness.

"Que es lo que pasa, ahorra?" Felipe grumbles. He sits up, handgun at the ready. "Come here, Kid," he says offhandedly and pats the bed before returning to his conversation with Reynaldo. If he is surprised by Kid's immediate compliance, he gives nothing away, just places a firm hand on his exposed shoulder and swirls his thumb.

"Sir, I thought you might like to know Celia is in Mr. Caleb's room. Do you have any orders?" He stands patiently in the dimly lit hallway.

Felipe's hand prevents Kid from leaving the bed. The boys Spanish has improved dramatically and is usually something for which he is praised...unless he's being an inquisitive little scamp. *"Easy, boy, Celia already has a protector."*

"But Felipe!" he decries in a mangled accent before lowering his voice. "That guy...he's...he..." *He cut off Tiny's head with a hunting knife.*

Felipe smiles warmly in response to Kid's concern for Celia. However, *"He* is none of *your* concern. Quiet now." It's an easy thing to collapse the younger man to the mattress by pulling on his supporting hand. It's a far more difficult task to ignore the spark of arousal catching fire in his stomach as Kid submits with little more than an indignant huff, but he has more pressing matters. *"Did she seem distressed?"*

"No, sir."

"Very well." Felipe yawns and sifts through Kid's hair, much to the boys chagrin. *"Thank you for alerting me. I'll*

take control of the situation. You may go." He waits for Reynaldo to shut the door before he turns toward Kid. "Your mistress is never far from the middle of things."

Kid sits up to grip Felipe's arm. "Go get her, Felipe. Please. Caleb is a monster." He swats the older man's placating hand away from his head. He doesn't want to be coddled while Celia is in danger.

"She's fine, I assure you. *Celia* is the monster under that particular bed. She's no doubt been planning this since Caleb arrived with Kitten." He sets his gun on the nightstand with a yawn. Kid eyes the weapon with wide eyes. "The safety's on."

"It's not that," he says firmly. "S'just kinda weird you kept a loaded gun in here…with me…while you're asleep."

Felipe rolls his eyes. "I know killers, boy. The most you could manage would be to give me a bump on the head." Kid's mouth falls open, agape with shock. Felipe shakes his head. "I never get tired of your expressive face."

"Whatever." Kid pouts. "Can we focus on Celia now? I don't get how you're just sitting here while she's alone with that asshole."

"Watch it, boy. I'm awake now and more than willing to distract you below stairs until Celia has concluded her business." Felipe waits for the words to sink in and for Kid to drop his shoulders. He may be young, but Kid is no one's fool.

"You want her to find out something?"

"I want her to do more than that." He rises from the bed and extends his hand toward Kid, who takes it without hesitation. They walk only a few steps to Felipe's desk, where he motions Kid into a chair and types his convoluted password to view his laptop's home screen. A few clicks later, they are watching Caleb go down on Celia in Kitten's room.

"Holy fuck! You've got a camera in there." Kid is scandalized by the invasion of privacy. "Does Celia know? Oh my God."

"Language, boy! Yes, she knows," Felipe says through a grin. Celia's legs are spread to their limit, her eyes closed in ecstasy as Caleb sucks and licks noisily between her pillowy nether lips. Celia's head rests in the lap of Caleb's virgin slave; Kitten does not appear pleased by the situation. In the days of Rome, Celia would have seduced the rulers of nations. It's Felipe's gain that their fates are tied. He is always looking to expand his empire.

His train of thought is disrupted by Kid's wince. On the screen, Kitten has just slapped Caleb and run off into the bathroom. He closes out the feed. "See that? She's jealous."

"So?" Kid asks seriously.

"If Caleb used Celia to solicit Kitten's jealousy, we can use it to our advantage. A man will do anything to protect that which he holds dear. I only need to know if this girl is more valuable to Caleb than his business relationships."

"What about Celia? Isn't she more important to you than your *business relationships*?" Kid does nothing to disguise his revulsion toward Felipe's cavalier attitude.

Felipe leans over until his nose nearly touches Kid's. "Whose idea do you think it was to get close to Rafiq's apprentice? Do not believe for a moment your mistress is incapable of intrigue. She knows more than you or I ever will about dealing with monstrous men. Understood?"

"I—I...yes, Felipe." He wants to leave it there and discovers he's unable. "But why?" Kid follows the older man back to bed and forgoes his floor pallet to climb beneath the blankets.

Felipe tucks the covers under Kid's chin. "Keep this secret and one of these nights, I'll tell you another." He knows it isn't the response the other man is looking for, but it's the only one he is willing to give. "Until then, tell me something about you I don't know."

Kid sighs. He isn't going to get more out of Felipe than the man wants to divulge, so he veers toward the path of least resistance. "My name's Andrew. Andrew William Benson. I don't think you've ever asked," he mumbles accusingly.

"Hmm," Felipe nods, "you were born in Yuma, Arizona to William and Sarah Benson. Your maternal grandparents are alive and living in Connecticut. Celia will have her hands full planning your birthday celebration in two months, and although you've been arrested for underage drinking, disturbing the peace, and criminal mischief, you've never spent more than a single night in a cell. Now," he pauses for effect, "tell me something I can't read from a police report." Kid's expression reads like closed captions for the hearing impaired: *Please stop talking before I start screaming.* Felipe runs his fingers through the boy's hair. "Why are you called Kid?"

Kid swallows several times before he can answer. "M-m-my dad," he chokes out. "In the army, he went by Wild Bill, you know...like the outlaw." His heart is pounding! He will *never* do anything to piss Felipe off—ever. "I was Billy the Kid."

Felipe smiles. "I have heard of them. Very sweet, boy."

"Yeah," Kid prattles on nervously, "Mama used to like to break out the pictures of me in my diapers and cowboy boots. I had a cap-gun on each hip." Felipe seems to genuinely appreciate the detail. Kid relaxes marginally.

"Do you shoot well?" Felipe asks.

"Nah," Kid smiles, "my mama never liked real guns. After she died, I never wanted to carry one. It used to drive Tiny crazy, 'cause it meant he had to watch out for me." Kid falls silent.

"Do you miss him?" Felipe inquires.

Kid nods shallowly. "Sometimes." He pauses. "It's more like…I forget to miss him and when I remember…I feel bad for wanting to forget again."

"When you miss him, do you ever think about revenge?"

Kid takes the time to consider the older man's question. Part of him does—want revenge against Caleb and the others—but then… "When I was twelve, my buddy Shaun Wiseman stole my girlfriend." The memory makes him laugh. "I was so pissed at him. He kissed her with tongue and everything—was more than I got from her. So I come home and tell Mama m'gonna kick Shaun's ass, and she said…" Kid finds himself getting a little choked up and takes a deep breath to settle himself, "she said revenge is for people who got nothing to lose." For the first time, Kid purposely seeks out Felipe's eyes. What does he want most? The voice in his head screams his answer loud enough to silence any errant thoughts of revenge. He knows his truth. "No, I don't ever think about things like that. What would be the point?"

Felipe experiences the oddest sensation. This boy does things to him, makes him feel like his heart is new. Following a few seconds of heavy silence, Felipe yawns. He leans over to press his lips to his bewildered lover's forehead. "Goodnight, Andrew. I want only pleasant dreams for you." He rolls over and shuts his eyes before the other man can reply. "I'm glad you chose my bed over the floor," he whispers.

55. Felipe/Celia

Despite the fact his goals are within reach, Felipe is none too pleased after his meeting with Caleb; Rafiq's apprentice is beyond arrogant. He suspects Caleb is high on Celia's affections and the idiotic notion he holds something over Felipe because of them—fool. And after all that Felipe and Celia have set in motion to give him a chance at love *and* his all-encompassing revenge. After all he's done to make sure they *all* get what they need in the end! Selfish—all of them.

Rafiq thinks he can fail to deliver his weapons on time and still demand his drugs. *Unconscionable!* Caleb sleeps in *his* house, under *his* protection, eats *his* food, and fucks *his* woman, and has *the gall* to give Felipe attitude. The look on his face when Felipe told him about the cameras…he'll find pleasure remembering it later, perhaps on Celia's face.

"Tell me, why do I allow her to sleep with other people?"
"She told me…that…um…she does it to get back at you…for…before."

Celia can be too brave!

And then there's Kid. He's…actually very sweet; Felipe nearly cracks a smile, but remembers he's on a mission. The boy has to earn his way, be it toward freedom or a new life. Felipe will collect what he is owed.

He barges into Celia's room full of malicious intentions. Kid, never having experienced Felipe's jealousy, is startled into dropping the sterling silver hairbrush he was using on his mistress' hair. Celia only smiles at Felipe through his reflection in her vanity mirror. *"Algún problema?"*

"Of course not. All is according to plan."

"Will he bring her to the party?" Celia is stoic and perfectly aware of the way her words slide between Felipe's ribs like satin covered steel. Last night, Caleb had her in a way her master will not allow himself, and then shamed her by throwing her out of bed afterward. It was a better result than she could have hoped for, because he had done it to spare Kitten's feelings. In fact, the entire display had been for Kitten. Caleb is a man in love with a woman he will not let himself have, and it reminds Celia so much of her own relationship that it makes her ache. Tomorrow night, Celia will see Caleb shamed in return *and* advance the plan.

"*Sí*," Felipe replies. His mind's eye replays the footage he watched this morning as he stares at Celia through the mirror. He sees Caleb's scarred back and tight body thrusting on top of his beautiful slave, his queen, the woman he's supposedly conquered and still doesn't own. He's seen her wide open legs and heard her pleasured moans thousands of times and felt nothing but lust. Other times, he feels as he does now, like a lovesick idiot low on self-respect.

"How did you get him to agree?" Celia says in thickly accented English. Her syntax is much improved thanks to Kid. She motions the young man—who has been standing nearby and seems to be working to make himself invisible by sheer force of will—toward the fallen hairbrush. She smiles at him brilliantly as he moves to pick it up.

Felipe intercepts his male lover and tugs the brush gently from his hand. The older man's eyes rake over Kid from toe to head and stop everywhere in between.

Weight, dense and full, settles low in his testicles. He licks his lips before he can help it; Kid mirrors the act. "How else? I blackmailed him. Why is he dressed this way?"

Celia takes possession of her hairbrush from Felipe's tight grip and begins brushing her hair. She watches her men intently in the mirror. Kid's blush nearly matches the color of his rouge tinted lips. Celia mentally pats herself on the back watching Felipe's hungry eyes roam over their boy. Yes, all is indeed going according to plan—*her* plan. They may have started this game to rid themselves of Rafiq's demands and their involvement in the pleasure trade, but it has quickly evolved to include other aims. There is another game she and Felipe have been playing for much longer, and she can sense checkmate is close. If she is successful, Kitten will have her Caleb, and Celia will finally have her master *and* a gorgeous boy for them to love and share without guilt. *"The dress is a little short for a proper lady in waiting—it's rare to find a woman so tall—but otherwise, he fits it well. Don't you think?"*

Felipe prides himself on awarding praise when it is earned. No one gets to him quite like Celia. She's clever, spiteful, stunning, stubborn, giving, loving, and brave; he worships her and she knows it. Part of him doesn't care if he ever gets to be with her as other men—they'll always have this; always have their games. *"You're exquisitely cruel, my dear."* He slowly reaches out to tuck a lock of Kid's hair behind his ear. He sighs. The younger man is another denied desire.

"Thank you, Master. I thought we might have some fun with his 'boy pussy'.*"* She smiles wickedly in the mirror. Felipe laughs. Kid's mouth falls open as he turns his head and looks at her with shock in his eyes and a plea written across his stricken face. *"I assume Master prefers it to mine."* Their smiles mirror one another in their reflections.

Felipe's jealousy falls away as though it never were. What does he care if Caleb challenged his manhood? He's a pawn, like Rafiq, like Reynaldo, and like Kid until he proves his loyalty. Felipe is a king. Celia is his queen. Jealousy is unbecoming their station. *"If my slave will only obey me and give herself to me, I would humbly accept."*

"Am I your slave, Felipe? If so, you don't require my permission for anything."

"Then by your own logic, all you need to free yourself is to accept me willingly."

Celia closes her eyes. A shiver races down her spine. *"A bird is not free simply because it can no longer see its cage."* Her eyes open and fix on Kid before they flick toward Felipe. "Aren't you going to unwrap your present?"

Felipe smirks. "Of course." He takes Kid unaware and manhandles him toward Celia's bed until the younger man is sitting in his lap with his legs over Felipe's wide knees, facing Celia.

"Hey!" Kid protests. "You don't have to toss me around, you know." He huffs indignantly.

"Shut up, and stop trying to close your legs," Felipe orders, pleased by Kid's immediate compliance. His eyes are firmly on Celia as he gently rucks Kid's dress and petticoats up over his legs and thighs until the mass of fabric rests just over his cock. He's tempted to look in the mirror to see if the boy is aroused, but he won't take his eyes away from Celia.

Celia inhales sharply at the sight of Kid, whose boyish, androgynous features make him even more remarkable as a woman. Her eyes quickly flit to his steadily plumping cock and then away. "He enjoys your touch." It makes her smile to see her young lover blush but open his legs marginally wider. He's such a good boy.

Felipe's hands run over Kid's body slowly and reverently. He takes the time to reach across his lover's chest and reach inside his bodice to pluck and tease his tender nipple—first one and then the other. He kisses Kid's neck gently and whispers how beautiful he is, how good and perfect, and how fervently he wants to bury himself in Kid's virgin pussy and pump him full. Whimpers, moans, and open-mouthed gasps hit the air unabashed.

Unable to resist the sinful temptation before her, Celia lowers herself onto her hands and knees to crawl between Kid's thighs.

"Oh God!" Kid shouts and tries to scramble away. There is nowhere for him to go, but his hands have a firm grip on Celia's hair to hold her back. "What the hell are you doing?"

"Put your arms around my neck, boy." Felipe's voice is deep and raspy against Kid's freshly sweaty neck.

"But...I *can't*," Kid pleads.

Celia gently eases Kid's fingers out of her hair.

"You can," Felipe says. He helps his good boy obey, because he knows he's scared of the unfamiliar. "Don't you love eating pussy? We do. And yours is gorgeous, boy—so tight and shy. Let her open it up."

Celia observes Kid gently toss his head from side to side in protest, but keep his arms wound tight around Felipe's neck. She nuzzles behind his smooth balls again to swipe her tongue over Kid's hole. She can feel his cock leap against her cheek with every graze of her tongue. There's a chorus of: "Oh...mmph...oh...oh...ah, ah, ah."

"That's it, my sweet boy. Tell me what you need. Do you want her to lick your pussy harder?" Felipe's young lover cries out and he accepts it as assent. "Stop teasing his pussy, Celia. Can't you see he's desperate?"

Celia moans and laps gently at the sensitive skin between Kid's balls and pink boy pussy. He tastes like almond soap and slightly bitter sweat. At Felipe's urging, she pushes her tongue further back and prods Kid's spit-covered hole. "Ohgodohfuckyeah. Yes!" Kid groans. He lifts his knees and her master does not disappoint, he is there to hold their lover's legs up and back instantly—like he was waiting.

Felipe's eyes are engrossed with the mirror. It's disgusting—filthy! He should be mortified by his and Celia's depravity—what they're doing to this beautiful creature. He should! But he isn't. He can never get enough of seeing his angelic-looking boy spread out on his lap with his dress rucked up, legs pulled back by Felipe's own masculine hands, and his cock pointed skyward leaking juice. Felipe grinds his cock into Kid's spine and nearly comes all over himself when Kid meets his eyes in the mirror, blushes, and mouths: "Kiss me." Felipe turns his head to fulfill his lover's timid request. His fingers squeeze the firm flesh of his boy's thighs at the first brush of lips. Kid has never asked for this, and Felipe feels the need to make it the best kiss he's ever bestowed. He nibbles gently at Kid's red lips and the boy opens for him; his warm breath hits Felipe's lips in rapid bursts. He slides his tongue in slowly; a surge of slick pulses out of his cock as Kid mewls and slides his own tongue against the older man's.

"Mmph...mmph," Kid whimpers into Felipe's mouth and rides Celia's tongue. When he pulls off to breathe, the first coherent words out of his mouth are to beg for a hand on his cock.

"Do you want to come, baby boy?"

"Uh huh." Kid rubs himself all over the older man.

"Do you like having your pussy eaten?"

"Sí, Felipe. *I want to come while she eats my pussy and you play with my cock. Please, Felipe. Don't make me beg."*

Felipe chuckles. *"Hold your leg up for me."* He moves one of his hands onto Kid's hot, fat erection and wraps his fingers around the velvety steel.

"Yeah," Kid moans and thrusts his cock in and out of Felipe's fist. "Fuck me *jusslikethat*. Ooooooooh."

Celia backs away from Kid's wet hole to admire her work; her boy is opening up so nicely. "No," she says, taking Felipe's hand off Kid's cock. She directs his fingers toward the boy's asshole and presses his thick index finger inside.

"Oh, God!" Kid shouts. Whether he realizes it or not, he's fucking himself on Felipe's finger and making the most wanton sounds Celia has ever heard.

"I can't take it anymore," Felipe surprises himself by saying. He speaks between open-mouthed kisses. *"Let me fuck your pussy. I'll make you feel so good—we both will. God! You're tight. Mmm…and hot. I have to have you, you understand? Say yes."* He teases Kid's lips with the tip of his tongue, hungry for more delicious pining.

"Mmmscared," Kid confesses. "You're so big," he groans. "'Sgonna hurt."

Celia slides her own index finger into Kid alongside Felipe, and the younger man spreads his legs as wide as he can manage. He fucks the air and his engorged cock slaps his belly with every thrust. *"You can take it, baby. I promise."*

"Will you…will you stop if I can't?" Kid pants as he rides the fingers in his pussy. Celia leans forward, mouth full of saliva, and rewets her and Felipe's fingers so she can slide another one inside. Kid freezes, but accepts the added stretch with a lascivious, decadent sound Celia will remember always.

"Does this hurt?" Celia asks. Kid shakes his head, eyes closed, mouth open, and toes curled inside his knee socks. *"Trust us."*

Kid nods. "'Kay."

Felipe doesn't waste a second. He gingerly slides their fingers out of Kid's hole, hooks the boy's legs with his arms and stands up. "Down on your knees, beautiful boy—face down on the bed." He kisses the younger man tenderly, helping him achieve his desired position while at the same time assuaging his inherent fear. Celia goes for the lube without having to be asked. She wants this as much as he does.

56. Kid

Felipe doesn't give him much time to adjust—simply throws Kid's dress up onto his back, spreads his ass cheeks, and sticks his tongue straight up his asshole. "Mmmm," he groans, and it makes Kid's insides vibrate.

Kid can't even speak. He's got a fucking tongue in his ass and it is *not* idle. A choked sound escapes him as he scrambles to hold on to something; he grips the comforter like it's the only thing keeping him tethered to the earth. Felipe flicks and sucks, bites and nibbles, and strokes and prods his keenly sensitive hole until Kid has no idea if he's moving his hips to get away or get Felipe's tongue deeper inside him.

Felipe pulls away abruptly and groans. Kid can feel his stare on his asshole and he instinctually clenches. "You trying to hide your pussy from me, boy? It isn't going to work." He swipes his tongue over Kid's hole.

"You should see yourself—pretty dress pulled up—pussy opening and closing with every breath you take." He shifts one hand onto his lower back and the other between his legs. "And this delicious little cock, so hard, leaking all the way down to your pretty white socks."

"Felipe," Kid gasps. He can feel his asshole flutter and his cock throb at the same time. If the older man doesn't stop talking, Kid's going to come before they get started.

Suddenly, Celia's hands are in his hair and pulling him up so she can sit on the bed in front of him. Kid groans and doesn't ask before his hands grip Celia's now naked hips to yank her down so he can get one of her hard nipples in his mouth. *"Sí, bebé. Un muchacho tan bueno."*

"Nnngh," Kid pines. He loves the taste of Celia's tits…and the feel of Felipe's hand massaging his cock and balls.

"I love your pussy, boy. Can't wait to stretch it out with my dick. Would you like that?"

Kid can't fight it. He wants this. He wants to be fucked and owned. He wants Felipe's big goddamn cock inside him and he wants to fuck Celia's pussy while he takes it. "Uh huh," he says around a mouthful of tit.

Felipe rubs his dick over his hole through the rough fabric of his pants and Kid arches his back so he can push back against it. "Look at you, such a whore for this cock, aren't you?" Kid nods his head and wriggles encouragingly. He's rewarded by the sound of Felipe undoing his pants and the hard, hot press of solid cock wedged in his crack.

"Ohhhhhhhhhgodyeahfuckit! Fuck my ass."

"Language," Felipe admonishes. It has to be a reflex by now.

Celia giggles, and Kid can feel himself blush up to his roots; his ears are hot. "You're a greedy boy."

Refusing to play the part of blushing virgin—even if he is—Kid musters his bravado. "Thought you like how greedy I am," he pants. "'Sides…if I'm gonna do it, might as well enjoy it."

Celia smiles and urges him on top of her. "Fuck me," she demands simply.

"You too?" Felipe chuckles and lies down on Kid's back to kiss Celia. Kid watches them both with building interest as Felipe nudges his asshole with the blunt head of his uncircumcised cock.

"He's a bad influence." She bites down on Felipe's bottom lip and sucks it gently before returning her mouth to Kid's.

"Ah…ohgod…oh, oh, oh." Kid can't decipher pleasure from pain as he's stretched open in miniscule degrees. His asshole burns, but his dick won't stop leaking and his hips won't stop rocking back and forth.

"Fuck me," Celia repeats, and this time, Kid complies instantly. He shoves into Celia's pussy until his balls smack her ass and he fucks. No rhythm, no strategy, only rut.

"Oh, God. Celia…mmm…so wet…*sofuckinwet.*"

"That's it, baby, take what you need and spread your pretty pussy for our master." Kid doesn't think; he does. He spreads his knees until his hips ache, so the older man can see all his intimate parts.

Felipe's cock pushes forward with firm pressure until something inside Kid gives way and the whole massive length of the older man's dick slides into him down to the balls. Kid shouts around the nipple in his mouth and stops thrusting. "Hurts, Felipe. Oh, God. Can you take it out, just for a little bit."

"Shhh," Felipe croons. "It'll pass, baby boy. Your pussy's never taken a dick before; let it get used to me."

Kid tries to do as Felipe says and stay still. Instead, he finds himself clenching and unclenching his muscles. With Felipe inside him and Celia beneath him, Kid can't keep his hips from making tiny movements. "Please," he begs, unsure of which of his lover's he's pleading with.

"Bésame," Celia whispers and slides her pussy up and down Kid's erection.

"Celia." Kid rests his head on her chest and palms one of her breasts. "It's too much. I'll come." She pays him no heed and drags him into a heated kiss.

"That's it, boy. Move your tight little pussy for me. Fuck yourself on your master's big dick and show me what a good boy you are." Little by little, Kid obeys until the combination of lube and Celia's pussy make him forget all about the pain and think only of his pleasure.

"I can feel you in my stomach. So big…can't believe it's all in my ass."

"Where? You know what I want to hear, boy."

Kid throws himself into the abyss. "Fuck my pussy harder, Felipe. I want to feel you come inside me." Felipe starts to slam forward on every thrust. "Big. Fucking. Cock. In. My. Pussy." His own balls tighten sharply and he panics. "I'm gonna come! Felipe, stop me…no…I don't want to…" He unloads into Celia's pussy with a sharp cry.

"Mother of God. I can feel you, boy. I can feel you coming inside my Celia." And then Felipe is coming inside him and the whole world is blurry at the edges. He holds tight to Celia and tries to focus on keeping himself open and loose as Felipe rides out his orgasm. Once it passes, the older man pulls out without preamble. He pushes a finger into Kid's fucked loose hole. "So beautiful."

"My turn," Celia pants. She pushes Kid's head down between her spread legs and practically forces his mouth onto her. It isn't the first time he's tasted his own come while going down on Celia, so he slides his tongue into her slippery folds, scooping up his own seed on his way to suck her clit the way she likes.

Under his mouth, Felipe worms his fingers into Celia's twat—three of them—so she's stretched taut. Together, they pleasure her pussy until she comes so hard Kid's own seed comes rushing back out. Kid swallows. Felipe licks his fingers clean.

Spent, sweaty, and freshly bashful—Kid pants against Celia's thigh while Felipe kisses his neck and Celia's wide open leg. "You taste amazing," Felipe says into his ear, and the elation Kid feels is proof he is accepting his cage.

57. Celia/Kid

Tonight is the night. Either Caleb will reject Felipe's request to have Kitten perform sexual acts with Kid in front of their guests—a clear indication he's in love with the girl—or he'll go through with it and Felipe will have to add Caleb to his list of collateral damage. Celia has a good feeling about how things will turn out.

"Do I really have to do this, Celia?" Kid stares at himself in the mirror with a grimace. He's naked but for a loin cloth. "This thing barely covers my junk, and the back!" He turns to view his bare buttocks. "Thongs are for chicks!"

Celia giggles from the bed. "You're gorgeous; you shouldn't be embarrassed. And *yes*, you must do this."

They will help Caleb get his revenge. Rafiq will undoubtedly die bloody. Felipe will get a new arms distribution pipeline and business partner to launder his heroin money through oil mining investments. Kid will be free of his enemies. Kitten will get her man, and Celia…well, she'll be bored again. It's fortuitous that Felipe's illicit activities provide so many opportunities for her to shine. Speaking of opportunities to shine—she makes her way over to Kid, who is still obsessing over his role and his nudity.

"Are you frightened?" she asks. Taking up the jar of flavored oil, she sets about her task of preparing Kid.

Kid expels the air in his lungs slowly. "I dunno. A little. I guess. I just…" He tugs at the front of his loin cloth several times before he accepts it isn't going to get any longer. "That girl and me have history. What if she doesn't wanna do stuff with me, and Caleb forces her? I'm not like that. And what if she *does* want to and Caleb gets pissed? I know what he's capable of, Celia. You didn't see what he did!" He shuts his eyes tight to ward off the vision of Caleb holding Tiny's head. He's trembling.

Celia wraps her arms around Kid. He bends his body to rest his head on top of hers. *"The past is powerful, I know, but do not let it dictate your future. Caleb has, and it's brought him nothing but suffering. He'll suffer unspeakably by the time our night is through, but you…you will never have anything to fear again."*

Several minutes pass before Kid is emotionally stable enough to stand tall. Felipe and Celia have asked him to do this, and for whatever reason, he doesn't want to let them down. He nods slowly, and as Celia resumes her ministrations, he speculates on his choices and how they've led him here. After his parents died, he'd made a slew of self-destructive choices. Hell, even before then, if he were honest. He'd been willful toward his parents and the weight of that guilt rested heavy on his shoulders after they passed.

Unable to please his parents, Kid tried his best to be an obedient son to his uncle, a man who had never wanted children. The guilt Kid suffered at the time, coupled with his crushing loneliness, had made it easy to drop out of school at fifteen, learn to ride a Harley, and follow Tiny. Shortly after, Kid discovered soft drugs, something Tiny encouraged, going so far as to push him toward dealing for easy cash. From there, Kid's decision to join the Night Devil's on their monthly runs into Mexico had been a foregone conclusion.

Kid supposes he has always tried to please someone: his parents, his uncle, and now Celia and Felipe. His parents loved him unconditionally, but it is a love he's lost. His uncle had felt responsible for him, but Kid had understood his uncle's love was reserved for his lifestyle. If Kid had been too young to ride a motorcycle, Tiny would have dumped him with his grandparents—complete strangers who never approved of his father. With Celia and Felipe, Kid knows he is wanted, if for no other reason than they won't let him leave. Somehow, they've given him the structure and affection he's been missing in his life and Kid knows exactly how to please them, because they never leave him to wonder. His world has become simple: obey or be punished. Kid decides simplicity offers its own peace.

Pulled abruptly from his thoughts, Kid grunts as Celia rubs oil over his cock and balls. He is sore from a tryst they had earlier, but he continues to eagerly anticipate release. Which, of course, has been Celia's intention all along. *Little bitch.* Kid smirks. At least he can still mouth off in his head.

Yes, there are times when Kid feels like a traitor for not holding on to his anger, but he always lets it go. Felipe can behave like a civilized man and Kid has come to think of him fondly, but he also knows Felipe can turn. Kid can never overlook the fact he's been brought to Felipe's home as a prisoner. The dungeon is his. Celia is his. The *rules* are his. There is no point in being angry, when the only person to suffer is him. For all the crappy choices Kid has made, letting his anger go feels right.

Celia reaches between Kid's thighs to playfully pluck the strap to his thong. Kid hates the outfit, but doesn't protest further. Just as he doesn't struggle against the clamps adorning his nipples. After all, Celia is wearing something similar.

Celia stands and circles Kid until she looks up at him. She smiles. "So beautiful." She traces Kid's bottom lip with her fingertip and he licks it.

"It tastes like honey," he says.

Celia's smile broadens. "I want you to taste sweet."

Kid chuckles and it sounds exactly like he feels—bewitched. "Yes, Celia."

Celia's smile falters. "Tonight will be hard." She runs her hands along Kid's arms.

"It always is, Celia." Kid tries his best to be comforting. It's the least he can do.

She pulls on his arm until he goes down to his knees before she wraps him in a hug. "No one will hurt you," Celia says softly. "I promise." Celia's English has improved significantly since Kid arrived. He feels grateful to Felipe for suggesting Celia and Kid practice English and Spanish together. Kid is damn near fluent—getting spanked by a ruler is one hell of a motivator.

Kid makes a feeble attempt at smiling. Celia is in no position to make promises, but the gesture is sweet nonetheless. *"Gracias,* Celia."

"De nada, Kid." They kiss for long minutes.

58. Celia

Things do not go exactly to plan, but the evening is a resounding success nonetheless. Rafiq, detained in Pakistan by his military obligations, is unable to attend Felipe's soiree.

Caleb *does* allow Kitten to go through with receiving and performing oral sex with Kid in front of their guests, but is so overcome by jealousy that he promptly takes her upstairs afterward and divests her of her virginity. Felipe, Celia, and Kid watch the video later that evening—Caleb thought he'd destroyed all the cameras, but failed to check the bed's frame—and they find the footage to be exceedingly titillating.

"I told you he wouldn't go through with it. Even the hardest hearts can be penetrated by Cupid's bow."

Felipe playfully rolls his eyes for Kid's benefit and the boy laughs. *"Very poetic, my dear, but Rafiq is still alive."*

"Yes," Celia says very seriously, *"but I have high hopes for a resolution."*

59. Felipe

For two blissful days and nights, Felipe's mansion is a pleasure palace. Caleb and Kitten scarcely leave their room, and Felipe, Celia, and Kid cannot get enough of watching them. Their voyeurism invariably leads to wildly erotic lovemaking. Two days and two nights—and then it happens.

It's the middle of the night when Felipe hears Reynaldo's sharp knock on the door; he never uses the keypad unless Celia is in danger. He succinctly informs Felipe that Rafiq and his men are waiting in the entryway.

"Tell Rafiq I am in the process of concluding some business and that you'll escort him to my study after you've helped them get settled. I want Rafiq in the guesthouse, not inside. Place his men in different wings. How many are they?"

"Rafiq, two guards, and…" Reynaldo pauses, avoiding Kid's inquisitive eyes, *"a slave."*

Felipe nods, grateful for Reynaldo's tact. There is no need for Kid to ever see his former lover or what has become of her. Celia has no sympathy for women who side with vile men, and Kid has no need to know that either. *"Understood. Go."* The moment the door closes, he addresses Celia, who is already pulling on clothing. *"Lock him in the panic room and warn Caleb his master is here. I'll keep them occupied in the study."*

"Felipe!" Kid cries out. He catches hold of the older man's wrist as he's attempting to get out of bed. "I can help! I don't need to be locked away in some panic room like a fucking child." He's out of bed and toe-to-toe with Felipe in an instant. He lords his two inches of height advantage over the other man.

On any other night, Felipe might enjoy Kid's newfound aggressiveness, but not tonight. One well-placed punch to the younger man's solar plexus and he's gasping for oxygen at Felipe's feet. "Language, boy! You can't kill a man with a cap gun." He steps over Kid's hunched body and retrieves his suit from the closet. "Do as you're told." He would prefer Rafiq did not have the satisfaction of having caught him unaware.

60. Celia

"Abra la puerta!" Celia growls outside Caleb's door. She doesn't like that Felipe is alone, even if her presence would do little to quell hostilities should they arise. She is many things, but an expert killer is not one of them.

The door opens and Celia bursts into the room and is greeted by Caleb and a knife trained on her throat. Kitten is on the floor crying by the side of the bed. There is a gun in her hand.

"What's going on?" Caleb snarls in her ear.

"I came to warn you. Rafiq and his men are here. They're downstairs with Felipe. They want to see you." Celia is sure to hold on to Caleb's forearm to keep pressure off of her throat.

"Caleb, let her go," Kitten sobs. "She came to warn us."

"We don't know, Kitten. She could be here to separate us."

Not for the first time, Celia witnesses Kitten's fire. The terrified girl raises the gun. "Let her go, Caleb. I'll keep her here."

Celia is on the verge of actually being afraid. She doesn't fear Kitten for a moment, but Caleb reminds her of a cornered animal and he has been known to behave erratically on occasion. His arm only loosens after Kitten pleads with him a second time. He keeps a tight grip on her nape.

"What's the plan, Caleb?" the girl asks with feigned calm.

"I need to go meet them."

"You can't! What if they're just waiting to kill you?"

"If everything is as Celia says, then there's no reason I shouldn't go downstairs."

"No," Celia interjects, "Felipe sent me to warn you."

"Why would he warn me?" Caleb insists on being skeptical.

"Felipe knows what's been happening between the two of you and hasn't said a word to Rafiq. He doesn't want to deal with the fallout. You've been here for months, instead of the few days Rafiq originally promised. The last thing he needs is bloodshed in the house," Celia snaps out in Spanish. Her eyes are beginning to water and she hates that she can't stop her voice from cracking. Soon. It will all be over soon, she reminds herself.

Caleb speaks to Kitten, "Stay here with her until I get back."

"Caleb, please don't go. Let's leave. Right now."

Celia cannot abide Kitten's wishes, no matter how much she wants the beauty to find happiness with her beast. Felipe needs Caleb. "I'll get her out if there's trouble," she says. Caleb stares at her incredulously. "There are passages in the walls. Felipe had them built in case we needed to escape. I'll get her out, I promise."

"Why would you?" Caleb asks, bewildered.

"Not for you," she spits. "I don't want her to suffer."

Caleb nods. "Thank you, Celia. I'm in your debt."

"If anything happens to Felipe, I'll be sure to collect," she warns, because threats are beneath her.

Caleb removes his hand from Celia's neck and grabs a shirt. "The library?" he asks. He leaves after a single nod of Celia's head.

Kitten breaks the silence. *"Caleb says Felipe's been watching us. He said you've been watching us. Why would either of you help?"*

"Felipe trusts no one, Kitten. I'm sorry I didn't tell you, but Felipe means more to me than you. I love him."

The girl is a sobbing mess and her arms shake with the weight of the gun in her hands. *"Did you really come to warn us, Celia? Is Caleb walking into a trap right now?"*

"I swear I came to warn you. As far as I know, Caleb is meeting his friends and nothing more. The worst thing you could do right now is panic." It's not *exactly* a lie. She meets Kitten's wary eyes and witnesses her open longing. She wants to believe. She *has* to believe.

"I believe you," she says and lowers the gun.

61. Felipe

"Celia?" Felipe knocks softly on Caleb's door. Uneasy about Celia's absence and Caleb's hesitancy to speak on the subject, he went to investigate the matter just as soon as he was able. After several long minutes, he repeats his query. "Celia?" He switches off the safety on his 9mm. Plans aside, he has to prepare for any deviation.

"I'm in here with Kitten," Celia says through the door. Her voice is strained, as though she's been crying and is now trying to hide it for Felipe's benefit.

"Why is the door locked?" Felipe rattles the knob. He's going to have keypads installed on all the doors as soon as possible, not just his and Celia's rooms.

"Caleb was worried," she says cautiously. "Where is he?"

"Downstairs with Rafiq. Open the door," he commands. It takes a while, but Celia gingerly opens the door. Felipe's heart clenches in his chest at the sight of a tearful Celia. He enters the room with his gun raised and his eyes vigilant.

"Tell her Caleb is all right," Celia says. She stands firmly between Felipe and the girl.

"Why have you been crying, Celia? What happened here?" Felipe's tone is deadly calm.

"Nothing, my love. I've just been keeping Kitten company." She attempts a rueful grin. *"She's scared, Felipe. Tell her Caleb is all right. She's worried about him."*

"He's fine," Felipe relents. Whatever has caused Celia such distress, he'll root it out later. For now, it's more important to him that he get Celia and Kid to safety. Whatever is to pass, it's going to happen tonight. "He and Rafiq are having a drink. He should be up here shortly. We can all wait for him," he says without lowering his gun.

"Why didn't he come himself?" Kitten frets.

"He couldn't, not without raising suspicions. As it was, *I* suspected something might be happening up here. Why were you crying, Celia?" Felipe asks again more softly.

"It's just girl talk, Felipe. Please don't make a fuss. She was terrified you were coming to hurt her, and it made me think about…" Celia's voice trails off. Slowly, she raises her hand to his cheek. *"Don't you remember what it was like in the beginning?"*

He does. He lowers his gun and presses a fervent kiss to Celia's forehead. *"I'm sorry she made you remember,"* he whispers, *"especially when I've tried so hard to make you forget."*

She reassures him. *"I have, Felipe. I promise you, I have."*

With that, Felipe returns his attention to the other woman in the room. "Go wash up, sweet girl. Your master should be coming back any minute, and I suggest you're ready for him when he does. You don't have much time together."

"What do you mean?" Her lip quivers.

Felipe is not without a heart, and this girl's boundless capacity for love and forgiveness prods at his idle conscience. "I wish there was more I could do for the two of you. I've enjoyed watching your relationship unfold. Good luck to you, Kitten." He means every word. He takes hold of Celia's hand and escorts her out of the room.

62. Kid

Kid has been beside himself with worry for several hours, waiting for Felipe or Celia to come and retrieve him…or for someone else to take him prisoner…or to hear that one or both of them has been murdered. He's angry with Felipe all over again for locking him away. His fingers rub the spot where Felipe's punch landed. He'll be tender for days.

Finally! A voice comes over the intercom; it's Felipe's. "Open the door, Kid. The code is 27-44-56-29." Kid wastes no time in punching in the code. Celia envelops him in her arms and sobs into his neck.

"Felipe? What's wrong?" Kid holds Celia to him as though she'll fly apart if he doesn't.

"There's no time to explain. Put on these clothes. We're leaving." Felipe brooks no argument and Kid knows better than having to be told twice when his master is this serious.

Still, Kid can't help but laugh as he zips his pants. "Did you have to bring me the lime green suit? I look like a gangly lizard." Celia laughs and sniffles, Felipe shakes his head, and the three of them rush out of the panic room.

Outside, Reynaldo is waiting for them in a pitch-black Cadillac CTS. Kid barely has time to admire the vehicle before Felipe's hand lands on his head and urges him into the backseat. Celia and Felipe slide in beside him. "Where're we goin'?" he asks. Despite his cooperation, Kid is more than a little nervous about the night's events. "What's going on, Celia? Why are you both acting so strange?" His mind quickly fills with all sorts of awful scenarios.

"Sit back," Felipe snaps. He places one hand on Kid's chest and reaches across for his seatbelt. Kid looks at Celia who is already with the program and latching her belt. Felipe makes sure hers is secure anyway before he sits back and secures himself. Reynaldo is seriously hauling ass down the driveway.

Once they're off the property, Reynaldo slows down and Felipe visibly relaxes. It's odd to see this side of the older man and he doesn't particularly like it. He prefers his master's haughty and over-confident demeanor because it makes him feel safe. Kid doesn't feel like he's out of harm's way right now. He rubs his abdomen.

"I apologize," Felipe says softly. He turns his face toward the window and reaches out to hold Celia's hand in her lap. "I shouldn't have hit you. Rafiq surprised me and I didn't want to discuss your safety." He meets Kid's eyes and says, "I won't ever do it again. A man has the right to choose his own destiny."

Everyone looks so grim. It makes Kid nervous. "Hey," he smiles, "just because I'm more of a lover than a fighter doesn't mean I can't take a punch. Ask Amanda Simpson; she punched me all through third grade and I still went out with her in junior high."

Felipe grins in spite of himself and covers his mouth. "I still should not have done it. You're my lover, not *just* my 'fuck toy' as you so eloquently put it once."

Kid scrunches his nose. "Gross! Do you have to say it like that? Lover? Sounds so...*old*." He winks at the other man, instantly pleased by the charmed look in his master's eyes.

"You're free." Celia's broken voice hits Kid's ears like a slap.

"Excuse me. What?" Kid takes Celia's free hand in his and squeezes. It isn't until Celia hisses in pain that he loosens his hold the slightest bit. "Celia, what the hell are you talking about?"

She turns her blotchy face toward him and looks up at him through spiky lashes. "Is that what you want?" She's so sad. Kid's heart feels like it's pulling apart in his chest.

"Celia," Felipe says in his 'I know what you're up to' voice. "Stop trying to manipulate him. *You know better than I do that if we don't give him his freedom, he'll resent us no matter how well we treat him.*"

Kid has never been more glad or miserable for his lessons with Celia. *"You're letting me go?"* He covers his face with his hands. The worst days of his life begin typically. Kid's parents went out for lunch and never returned. His uncle went out for a beer and wound up with his head separated from his shoulders twenty-four hours later. The normality of the events leading up to each catastrophe has always sat heavy in his gut. This morning, he woke up to Celia's warm kisses and Felipe's hot mouth on his skin. He was happy.

"Isn't that what you want, boy?" Felipe asks. "Your freedom?"

"Yeah...I guess." *Please. Don't send me away.* Celia thrusts her face onto his chest and sobs. "Celia—"

"—We'll travel by car for a few hours to a private airstrip. Reynaldo can take you anywhere you wish," Felipe says. His tone gives nothing of his emotions away. Except...Kid can see how hard he's gripping Celia's hand. He can't look away.

Kid has been wary of ever feeling safe and secure. Wary of the happiness those things might bring him. Terrified of what might happen if he ever found himself completely alone.

Terrified of *this* fucking moment.

"Boy. Look at me," Felipe says.

Kid calls upon every lesson Felipe and Celia have taught him. He meets the other man's eyes without sobs or protests. He sits, quiet and patient, as *this* world crumbles around him too.

"Do you remember what I asked you when we met in the dungeon?"

Kid answers steadily. "You asked me what I wanted most in the world."

"Do you remember what you said?"

Kid doesn't dare look down toward Celia who is still sniffling on his chest. Felipe has a fondness for poetry, and Kid has to hand it to him—this shit is poetic. He's going to give Kid his freedom now that he doesn't want it anymore. Felipe has somehow found a way for him to provide his own send off and break his own fucking heart in the process. "I said..." he wipes at a tear that has somehow escaped, "I said I wanted to go home."

"Yes, and you said you couldn't because there is no one left to love you," Felipe whispers.

"That too."

"Do you still believe you're unloved?" Celia's shuddery words are softly spoken against him.

Kid shrugs. He's getting fed up with this shit. "I guess."

Felipe stares at him for several minutes as though he's trying to decipher truth from fiction. "I'd wager you're wrong," he says simply.

Kid can't take any more. "What are you saying?" He glances first at Felipe, then Celia. "You want me to go? I'll go. You want me to stay? I'll stay. Stop being so shy all of a sudden because we all know how ridiculous it is and tell me what to do! You've been doing it for months. Nothing new."

Felipe kisses his teeth but a smile lurks in his expression. "I'll take your desire for instruction under advisement, boy. For now, I'm *asking* you: Will you *choose* to stay with Celia and me? Will you choose us? Will you give us the chance to love you?" There is a hint of yearning in the question.

Simultaneous emotions bombard Kid's every synapse. He's falling and flying. Terrified and yet elated. He wants to cry and to laugh. But he settles for spewing out a stream of consciousness. "Fuck!" Kid exclaims. "Why the fuck didn't you just say *that*? I thought you were getting rid of me! I'm over here choking down my dinner so at least I have something in my stomach when you toss me out. I'm wondering how I'm going to live without you guys, and the whole damn time, you never said I can stay?"

Felipe laughs heartily and pulls both his lovers close to him. He kisses both their heads. "Language, boy." He pecks the younger man's lips when Kid lifts his head. "Such a filthy mouth."

Celia wipes her eyes and grins. She kisses Felipe, and then Kid. "We'll just have to remind him of his manners."

Kid laughs. "Yeah, I guess you better." He boldly reaches beneath Celia's dress to bury his fingers in her slippery pussy. Seconds later, he takes those fingers and slides them into Felipe's mouth before he kisses the older man senseless.

They unbuckle their seatbelts because:

Celia can be too brave.

Felipe can't tell her no.

And Kid is determined to obey.

-Fin-

WONDERFUL NEWS!

THE DARK DUET HAS BEEN OPTIONED FOR TV

They've asked CJ Roberts to act as Executive Producer which means they want her input on how to translate from a book medium to television. Yay!

HOWEVER, nothing happens overnight and the road ahead is going to be arduous. CJ asks for your continued support as we try to make this TV series a reality. A lot can happen between the option purchase and selection by a network. PLEASE, PLEASE, PLEASE, help make this happen by sharing the news, posting reviews, and encouraging everyone to:

Visit
www.care2.com

Search
Please create a TV Series based on
THE DARK DUET by CJ Roberts

SIGN THE PETITION

ABOUT THE AUTHOR

CJ Roberts is an independent writer. She favors dark and erotic stories with taboo twists. Her work has been called sexy and disturbing in the same sentence.

Her debut novel, *Captive in the Dark*, has sold over 150,000 copies and is the first of three books in her bestselling and award winning series *DARK DUET*.

She was born and raised in Southern California. Following high school, she joined the U.S. Air Force in 1998, served ten years and traveled the world.

She is married to an amazing and talented man who never stops impressing her; they have two beautiful daughters.

Stalk her:
www.aboutcjroberts.com

Made in the USA
San Bernardino, CA
14 November 2014